MURDER

WILL

OUT

MURDER

WILL

OUT

Dorian Yeager

An Elizabeth Will Mystery

St. Martin's Press
New York

Design by Junie Lee

Library of Congress Cataloging-in-Publication Data

Yeager, Dorian.
    Murder will out : an Elizabeth Will mystery / Dorian Yeager.
      p.   cm.
    "A Thomas Dunne book."
    ISBN 0-312-11388-9
    1. Women detectives—New Hampshire—Fiction   I. Title.
PS3575.E363M87   1994
813'.54—dc20   94-32369
                                                    CIP

First Edition: December 1994

10 9 8 7 6 5 4 3 2 1

*For Dad: the man who taught me
to haul, shoot, and shut my traps.*

ACKNOWLEDGMENTS

Steve, the piano man on his white charger;
Bernie, and the Miss Elle's gang;
the friends who heard it all a thousand
times without screaming; and, always,
Fran Lebowitz and Reagan Arthur.

ONE

"RED SKIES IN the morning, sailor take warning."

Elizabeth Will looked over from where she was looping a trap line past the winch connected to the diesel engine, and thought, *Easy for you to say. Who the hell is sailing here, and who the hell is sitting?*

Elizabeth's pale green eyes briefly swept toward the horizon beyond the burly man expounding ancient wisdom from where he hunkered on the sloppy rail of the lobster boat. Irritation and the rough offshore wind raised a youthful glow on her thirty-three-year-old face. The ruddiness gave a vigorous and stubborn appearance to what, on dry land, was a studiously composed beauty. Too fair to earn a living on the water, looking too fine-boned for physical labor. But there she was, anyway.

The breaking dawn was, indeed, a deep bloody wash. Elizabeth's finely calibrated brain ticked. She reminded herself that her palette was nearly out of the same shade of paint as the threatening sky. Alizarin crimson. She would pick up another tube as soon as she had showered and finished cringing. As with all red watercolors, the tube of pigment was going to cost her plenty; and paying for it meant even more time spent trapped on a small boat with the man who drove her closer to round-the-bend, pound-the-walls crazy than anyone else in the world.

Elizabeth tried to warm the creeping chill in her shoulders with the knowledge that the catch had been good so far that morning, and boat price for lobster was decent that week. She'd get by somehow, leading an "alternative" lifestyle, but, oh, what a way to subsidize art.

Keeping alert so as not to get tangled in the pile of rope coiled at her feet, she studied the way the lowering sky wept into the horizon, mixing the tints in her mind to get precisely the correct tone.

Damn. She was out of Payne's gray, too.

The art season kicked off with her one-woman show coming up next week, and she would have to hang at least five more paintings than she had finished to make any kind of presentable display for the regional art association—not to mention the often disagreeable tourists who (along with their most agreeable travelers' checks) frequented such places. No doubt about it: lower-middle-class stank and poverty reeked. Elizabeth chastised herself for not having chosen her parents with more care.

"Come in, Rangoon." The man on the rail interrupted her thoughts. "We've got another thirty pots to haul."

"We?" she questioned. "What we?" She wrapped the sodden rope twice around the clumsy scuba glove on her right hand, and turned to her father. Frank Will's weathered face settled into a familiar and infuriating look of benign condescension. Elizabeth was certain he did it on purpose, but it was just the way his face fell naturally.

"You signed on as helper." He lifted himself from his precarious perch and lumbered to the cooler under the canopy. "So, help already." He reached into the grimy white Styrofoam and pulled out a beer. "Want one?"

"At five forty-five in the morning? No, thanks," she replied.

The cadmium–yellow rubber coveralls that encased her wiry body squeaked with moisture, reminding her to wonder how her supply of *that* paintbox color was holding out.

A freshening breeze blew from beyond the shoals, ruffling her strawberry-blond hair where it had escaped from the hood of her slicker. A wet-cold shiver ripped down her arms, which were straining at the weight of the lobster pot and water resistance. The winch took a lot of the drag, but Elizabeth was developing some rather impressive biceps nonetheless. Rather than consider the possibility that she was beginning to resemble her father in any way—physically or (God forbid) mentally—she shook out the cramps and stretched her long fingers. Two unfortunate features of the life of a watercolorist were overdeveloped arms and back, the result of lugging around stacks of paintings ballasted with frames and glass. Commercial fishing was not doing anything to soften her up, either. She reminded herself that she was an artist (didn't believe it any more than she ever did) and put her muscle into the job at hand.

With a final heave, she threw the buoy into the boat, holding the rope around her left arm, and grabbed the trap with her right. A quick release and her rubber-clad fingers clasped the slatwork of the pot and yanked it onto the rail.

Five lobsters, tails coiling and whacking, clamored hopelessly in the trap. Green crabs scrabbled over the bloated remains of a redfish hanging in waterlogged shreds from the sharp bait spike. Any resemblance to Elizabeth's life was strictly coincidental. She tried not to consider that the fact that the connection came to her made a point to the contrary.

Sucking down the last of his beer, Frank said, "Looks like two keepers," as Elizabeth reached for the gauge that would confirm—or, she hoped irritably, contradict—her father's guesstimate. The heavy hooked aluminum measuring instrument was pitted from the salt air. She placed one curved end at the biggest lobster's eye and

3

laid the other down the green crustacean's back. The juncture of the tail was a good quarter inch beyond the gauge's reach: a keeper.

Frank's eyes were still better than his disposition, she found when she measured the second lobster, which was also a legal take. The other three lobsters were "shorts," too small, according to state law, to keep.

Elizabeth jammed wooden pegs into the cartilage of the legal lobster claws and tossed both "chickens"—about one and a quarter pounds apiece—into a large plastic holding tub in the center of the deck before she started throwing the smaller lobsters back overboard.

"Hey, hey, hey," Frank objected, grabbing one of the undersized tidbits from his daughter's hand. "These young, tender ones have 'lunch' written all over them. I told Jesse to tie up with us at the islands for a clambake."

She grabbed the illegal catch from her father's big hand and lobbed it twenty feet out into the gray water. "I have to open the gallery," she said before the picnic idea started to sound too good to her. "I can't spend valuable tourist-season hours playing with you and your politically incorrect scum buddies." She pitched the last an extra ten feet out to further convince herself. "Not to mention paying the fish and game boys fifty bucks apiece for half-pounders."

Unruffled, Frank returned to his seat on the lee side of the old boat. "Have it your way." Elizabeth heard the pop of another beer can. "But we *never* get caught." He tapped his graying head. "Stealth. Guile. A larcenous nature. Besides"—he took a healthy swig of beer—"unlike me, you're not getting any younger, and Jesse—gawd save him—likes you."

"So does the dog." Elizabeth grabbed three of the larger green crabs from the webbed head of the trap and systematically smashed their backs against the sharp wooden corner of the cage. Better them than Frank, she guessed.

4

Just about the last thing she needed was another discussion of her unmarried state and Jesse Kneeland's hound-like willingness to correct that sad situation.

Jesse was a fine man: loyal, steadfast, and hardworking. What in the world would Elizabeth Will want with a man so much like herself? Except, of course, that Jesse Kneeland was also (in Elizabeth's somewhat unkind opinion) dumb as a bucket of hair.

Clutching the shattered crab bodies expertly between splayed fingers, Elizabeth slammed them onto the bait hook, dropped the closure, secured it, and chucked the trap back over the side. The line attached to the buoy played out neatly. Despite the two bricks used for weight, the wood-slatted apparatus slid beneath the surface of the water lazily. Currents made the trap sway like a ballroom dancer, smoothly, side to side, and out of sight in the murky Atlantic.

Forcing the Jesse issue—as he always did—Frank said, "The dog doesn't own her own fleet of fishing boats." He tossed both his beer cans overboard, pulled out his stainless-steel thirty-eight revolver, and dead-eyed a shot apiece into the floating cylinders. Both went down without a sound. "Recycling in action!" Frank announced with childlike satisfaction, knowing how his juvenile displays of marksmanship annoyed his firstborn. Actually, it was his sheer, never-ending perversity that really annoyed her, as Elizabeth never ceased to remind him and he never ceased to ignore. Frank was as proud of his prickliness as he was of Elizabeth's.

Which was probably the character trait that had her withering on the vine instead of solidly, irrevocably married forever and ever like her sister. On the other hand, she was not exactly meeting a lot of men around the water cooler at the office, either. She throttled the engine and pointed the peeling hulk of the craft farther out to sea and toward the deep-water shelf half a mile away from the upcoming island's shore. Deceptively white-hot sparks reflected off the choppy surface as the sun sniped over the horizon. Liz felt the beginning of a dull headache. She either needed a long vacation far, far away from her father or, failing such inconceivable perfection, a full eight hours' sleep.

"If you get your way," Frank said, "I guess there'll be recycling bins floating around out here, along with the hookers and gangsters."

"We had our say last night. I'm not going to argue with you again this morning, you recalcitrant old fart." Elizabeth could feel herself being sucked into another "battle of the Wills" and hit the verbal brakes.

Frank, being Frank, put the pedal to the metal.

"Nice talk," he commented blandly. "Hooker and gangster talk. Never thought I'd see a daughter of mine inviting Jimmy Hoffa and the Mayflower Madam into our living room for by-jeezus tea."

"Since when did the isles become our living room?"

"The minute the privateers hauled anchor and you pretty-in-pink liberals took over the Town Meeting." He stretched and clasped his hands behind his head. "I just want to know, after you legalize gambling and prostitution, do I get to jack deer and rake clams off season?"

Elizabeth pushed the throttle forward for more speed from the thirty-year-old boat—and to keep her hands from wrapping around her father's neck. She struck back.

"Who bitches and complains about taxes going up, huh? Who? Seven days a week, twenty-four hours a day? Who?"

"Me," Frank answered calmly. "As head of the family, it's my job to express dissatisfaction."

"Well, as woman of the house, my job is—if possible—to provide peace and quiet for myself and the general public. And," she punctuated, "if Dovekey Beach taxed legal gambling and prostitution, I wouldn't have to listen to you piss and moan about government extortion."

6

Frank grinned at his favorite daughter's annoyance. "Would anyway," he said.

"Won't even allow me naive hope, will you?"

"Nope." He opened another beer. "Respect you too much." And he did—in his way. And his daughter knew it—in her way. Unfortunately for both of them, it was the same way.

Elizabeth was seized with the urge to resort to a blue streak of profanity, but wouldn't give her father the pleasure. The seacoast was being buried in property taxes after the closure of military installations in the area. Al Jenness's proposal to convert the closer shoal islands into the new Las Vegas of the Northeast was genius.

Al was not the seacoast's most successful businessman for nothing. One month's tax on legalized sin would cover the Dovekey Beach town budget for the year.

Elizabeth stared accusingly at the disputed cluster of rocky islets growing larger across the bow of the *Curmudgeon II*. What a waste of revenue. The three boils of scraggy acreage seemed to stick their tongues, of skeletal buildings and sedge grass, out at her. The markers of long-abandoned burial plots disturbed expanses of desolate turf.

Overall, not a bad place to observe eternity's sunrises, though. Quiet, unlike life.

The Town Meeting the night before had been particularly vituperative. Elizabeth, her sister, Avis, and a few dozen other concerned citizens had fought for casinos and cathouses against Frank Will and an equal number of morally righteous opposition cohorts. The passion and furor of the altercation were due in large part—as always—to the Machiavellian ministrations of Avis and Elizabeth's dear old dad.

If Elizabeth said economic measure, Frank counterclaimed moral turpitude, and then proceeded to support the correctness of his position with a merciless assault of browbeating rhetoric.

The debate at Town Hall had everything: hurled invective,

badgering, threats. All in all, pretty much like an evening at Frank and Elizabeth's home, except with a cheerleading section.

"You're not taking this personally, are you?" Frank asked. He looked as though he cared.

"Personally? That I was called an artsy-fartsy dilettante n'er-do-well by my own father?"

"No," Frank said, relieved by her snotty answer. "That you and your buddies are going to lose."

"What makes you think we're going to lose?"

He looked smug. "Because I *always* win."

And generally that was the truth. But there were others, too, Elizabeth reminded herself, who wanted New Hampshire to remain the last state in the Union with neither a sales tax nor an income tax. In this altercation, Town Selectman Al Jenness was firmly entrenched on Elizabeth's side, and he was a man to be reckoned with: wealthy, intelligent, and nearly as belligerent as Frank.

Now why had Al gone and gotten himself married? Elizabeth imagined her father's chagrin at having a son-in-law exactly like himself. It would have been worth marrying Al just for that, though she had thought of some additional perks during several sleepless nights alone. She really ought to shop around for someone marriageable and go for the long-term thorn in Frank's side instead of an adulterous hit-and-run. It was an option to consider. Might be good for her complexion, too.

She set her jaw. Steering with her left hand, she tucked a long pine pole with a nasty metal hook under her right arm, and slowed the vessel. In a clean, practiced sweep, she reached out with the hook and entangled the rope just beneath the Day-Glo orange and black of one of her father's marker buoys. She was determined to avoid bloodletting that morning.

"Jesse's a man of substance." Frank raised the red flag again. He was getting bored and wanted a rematch.

"Two boats—one in dry dock—do not a fleet make, Father,"

Elizabeth grumped. If ever there were an object lesson to discredit marriage, it was the years she had spent watching her parents hammer each other with their opposing temperaments and ambitions. She threw the boat into neutral.

"Just looking out for your best interests," Frank murmured, unruffled.

"Shit," she spat, making her preliminary pull at the buoy with the gaff. It budged a foot of line and held as stubbornly as the woman at the other end.

"I beg your pardon?" Frank was resorting to good manners. A transparent ploy.

"We're snagged," she explained.

Frank examined his gun thoughtfully. "Want to shoot a mako shark, bleed it, and stock the freezer?" He was trying to make amends. Barbecued mako with raspberry sauce was one of his daughter's favorite dinners, though she denied it on principle, and Frank was feeling especially gastronomically creative.

"I"—she yanked—"do"—and yanked again—"not."

Unperturbed, Frank wandered over to stand at her side. "Having that upper-body strength problem again, dear?"

Elizabeth considered the penalties for parental abuse in New Hampshire, bit back her witty rejoinder, and handed Frank the cold, slimy buoy. "Yes."

Let her father wrestle with the snagged trap. Maybe it would wear him down a bit. She doubted it, but handed over the rope anyway.

He tucked the revolver into the waist of his heavyweight khakis and looped the hemp around his knotty forearm.

"Son of a whore!" Frank cursed at his first try to bully his catch to the surface. "How the by-jeezus did you do this?" Veins stuck out at the sides of the big man's leathery neck. Elizabeth ignored his discomfort.

"Need some help?" she asked innocently.

"Think you've by-gawd helped enough," Frank commented, his face going boiled red as he groaned along with the noisy winch. Once the line started playing upward, he struggled less (or faked better), and shot his daughter his infamous crooked eyebrow of self-sufficient disdain. "Would have been a shitload worse if those 'biostitutes' out there on Piscatawk Island had lopped the lines again," he groused, pulling the polyester rope, standing on the slack, and pulling again.

Elizabeth looked to her right, forty yards to the state-of-the-art Tinker Toy construction on fifteen-acre Piscatawk Island.

At the turn of the century, Piscatawk and the other large island had been flourishing upper-class resorts. A spate of fires had reduced the lavish Victorian hotels to rubble. Being seven miles out to sea had not made for particularly efficient and timely fire department intervention, and the owners had been smart enough to know it, shoulder their losses, and bolt. Until three years ago, Piscatawk had been left to host the legendary ghosts of seventeenth-century pirates, seagull droppings, and the occasional picnic. That was when an environmental group with more money than public relations acumen had built its research station.

With the blessing of a one-term Democratic governor, the Eternal Sea Group—ESG—had set up eminent-domain housekeeping behind a perimeter fence that did homage to the old top-security Portsmouth Naval Prison. Except the architecture was not nearly so elegant.

The only noises wafting over the little boat were the screaming of gulls and the steady whir of the engine and winch. Windows in the ESG dormitory buildings remained the same dull, flat gray as the cold water below. Too early for the academics to be rising and shining, Elizabeth dourly supposed. The razor-wire pillow that was moved aside when the scientists were up and about still barricaded the path at the dock testified to their sleeping state.

"All right," Frank ordered, snapping Elizabeth from her

thoughts. "Make yourself useful and help me get this damned beast on the rail, so we can finish the rest of the run."

"Yes, sir, Cap'n Queeg, sir," she answered without a hint of joshing, and went at it with muscle if not enthusiasm. She was well aware that if Frank had a heart attack, she would only end up having to nurse him back to his usual bad temperament. She secured the toes of her rubber overalls in the slatted woodwork of the deck and folded herself double over the side. The foam diver's gloves caught a neat hold on the fiber trap line.

She pulled slack at the water surface as her father coiled the unnaturally white worm of rope to her left on the rail. Her hands were going to be a chapped mess for the opening of her show, but there was no helping it.

Finally the line played up easier. Her hands were going numb in the clammy cold. Losing patience at wasted painting time, she reached deeper and deeper beneath the chop to get a faster pull on the line.

The rising sun illuminated dapples of plankton-green ocean. Elizabeth's mind wandered as it often did during physical labor. The skin on her face was a crackled dry mask from the salt spray and the welcome warmth of the daylight. *Mix a little Hooker's green and burnt sienna,* she idly thought. *That'll give me about the exact shade to—*

A visceral grunt escaped her chapped lips. Whatever they'd snagged was a monster. She hoped it wasn't another of the World War II torpedoes that still got hooked after so many years of lying in deadly wait. If it was a torpedo, she prayed to God it wasn't German. The American-made missiles were most often duds, but more than one lobsterman had gotten himself blown to chum by a forty-odd-year-old Reich-dropping.

You had to hand it to the Krauts, Liz thought, when it came to long shelf life. If she ever got rich enough to buy a new car, she was shopping for a Mercedes.

At that moment her arms throbbed so intensely, she wasn't sure she even minded the prospect of an inconvenient shrapnel incident. After all, burial was not called being "laid to rest" for no reason. Still, when she finally made out the gray-beige of the familiar pot materializing through the hazy water, she shook with a small shudder of relief.

Impatient with herself, she gave a last frustrated, grunting pull.

The bloated corpse broke the surface with a sucking blurp, the suction hawking a bubble of brine into Elizabeth's open mouth. She froze in position, salt water drooling down her chin, her mind rejecting what her senses shrieked.

Clutched in the black and yellow of her Neoprene glove were the lobster-gnawed remains of a dead man's wrist. The clean-shaven throat was neatly wound into the funnel neck of webbing inside the lobster pot, the pink scalp pressed tightly against the lace of the "parlor room"—the middle section. One stripped-clean skeletal claw seemed to tear in death at the wooden mask; the other lolled in the uninterested swell.

Never had the word "trap" carried so much meaning for Elizabeth Will.

TWO

It was half an hour before the Coast Guard launch joined the *Curmudgeon II*. Jesse Kneeland had been monitoring the citizens band channel and beat the shore patrol to the scene by twenty minutes.

The ocean floor was too deep to drag anchor effectively, so the younger fisherman tied up to Frank's boat. Elizabeth and the two men secured the body of Selectman Jenness floating in its crate to the winch side of the *Curmudgeon*. Jesse tried to get Elizabeth to turn away or, better, jump over to his boat, but she refused for no reason other than she wanted someone who cared to tend one last time to Al.

And then all she could focus on was trying to remember what Al's hands had looked like the night before. Softer than hers, certainly. Smaller than Frank's, more welcome than Jesse's. Fully fleshed then, last night.

When the necessary job was complete, rather than accept awkward comfort from Jesse or gruff pep talk from Frank, Elizabeth grabbed a beer from the battered cooler aforedeck and sat aft, feet dangling over the side.

More at a loss than usual, Jesse kept his looming distance;

Frank approached his daughter only once, to replace her empty beer can with an ornate silver hip flask of brandy. She crushed the empty can in her stronger right hand, tossed it in the water, slipped her father's thirty-eight from his waist band, and drove a bullet through the crumpled heart of her old friend Mr. Budweiser. Jesse let out a startled noise as the can skipped twice and sank.

Elizabeth alternately put the brandy to her lips and compulsively kneaded the deep etching on the flask with her thumbs. Were Al's fingers long and narrow like hers? She thought not.

"Well," Frank said as much to himself as to Elizabeth after twenty minutes of waiting, "at least you didn't barf. Gotta give you that." He returned to the cabin end of the boat to join Jesse, whose ears had turned a shocking red in the cold wind. Each time he pulled up his hood, the wind snapped it back. Frank pulled the collar of his flannel shirt up inside the neck of his parka for extra protection and yanked his battered Stetson farther down on his head.

Finally the Coast Guard cruiser *Frank Jones* idled off the starboard side of the *Curmudgeon II,* keeping a respectful distance from the bobbing corpse. Within another minute, a very tall, angular woman in a smaller power craft threw a line to Elizabeth and scrabbled deftly aboard. Had her father not been watching her, Elizabeth would have wept with relief.

"You okay, Biz?" asked the brunette, using the nickname she'd given Elizabeth somewhere in the throes of the fourth grade.

"Actually, I had hoped you were Sean Connery," Elizabeth gamely answered. Ginny Philbrick threw her long arm around Elizabeth's shoulder and gave her old buddy a quick, businesslike hug. At that moment, the sun made its presence fully known and raised the temperature dramatically. Ginny unzipped her khaki parka, revealing the dark blue trousers and shirt that were her uniform. The gold shield over her pocket announced what everyone aboard already knew: "Chief of Police, Dovekey Beach, New Hampshire."

Ginny checked Elizabeth's eyes, but saw none of the signs of shock that would be expected in someone who had recently pulled up a dead body. She questioned her old friend in the only way she was accustomed to: "So, you got me a present?"

As Elizabeth pointed to the rope pulled taut through the winch at the fore, the Coast Guard launched a fifteen-foot wooden dory to join them. Arm in arm, the two women walked over to the patient Frank and Jesse under the canopy. Though a far cry from hysterical herself, Elizabeth marveled at Ginny's no-nonsense professionalism. Of course, six years with the New York City Police Department would have ground away some of those innocent New Hampshire edges—and Ginny hadn't been a wuss even as a child.

Elizabeth could not count the number of times Ginny had trotted off the basketball court shaking her dark clipped head in annoyance at a mere broken finger or two, flicking perspiration at the other players as though absolving them of their sins of lesser coordination.

"Whatcha got for me, Frank?" Ginny asked, slipping her arm out of Elizabeth's. Jesse tried to move into Ginny's place but was gently rebuffed. He, of course, took this as encouragement. Elizabeth warmed her hands at the door opening to the boat's engine, thinking how much more fragile the men looked than the women.

If she had had a mirror handy, she would have rethought that evaluation. The sprinkling of freckles on her nose stood out like rusty blotches across the putty-colored palette of her face. The sun's warmth did nothing to coax the blue cast from her full lips.

Frank crossed his arms, brazen machismo resurfacing, and answered.

"The usual. A floater that got sunk." Elizabeth could tell that her father was shaken, though after thirty years of fishing this was not the first drowning victim he'd helped recover. Not even the second or the third. Of course, this was the first one that had been crammed into its own gift box.

There was a hollow thunk as the Coast Guardsmen lashed on to the peeling aft of the *Curmudgeon*.

"Local or tourist?" Ginny asked no one in particular as she leaned over the side for a closer look at the corpse.

"Al Jenness," Elizabeth answered, handing Ginny the flask of brandy. She wiped her nose with the sleeve of her slick coverall, which did nothing at all to help; in fact it made her nose even colder and wetter for her trouble.

"Holy shit," Ginny muttered, taking a long swig of cold liquor and looking down at the body. "Surer than shit," and she tipped the flask back one more time. She turned when she sensed a new presence behind her and saw the windburned face of a young Coast Guard lieutenant over her shoulder. The pink flush across his cheeks drained to a chartreuse pallor.

With a graceful sweep of her arm, Ginny directed the green officer to the opposite side of the boat. "Over the side, kiddo." The uniform remained immobile. Ginny nudged him to the lee. "The *other* side."

Being an officer and a gentleman, the lieutenant did as ordered, and lost his breakfast downwind from the evidence.

After the young man's dry heaves subsided, Ginny turned down Jesse's gallant offer to hoist the late selectman onto his boat, and requested that the Coasties transport the deceased back to shore.

Always best to keep violent death in the hands of professionals, she reasoned. Especially the hands that had the storage space.

The lieutenant was happy to have his men comply.

The men weren't quite so thrilled.

THREE

Dr. Ben Ryan was waiting impatiently at Dovekey Harbor. The last of the old-fashioned house-call physicians paced in a small circle, smacking his arms to his chest from time to time to keep warm.

A chain-smoking man in his early seventies does not have the best circulation in the world, the doctor admitted to himself, and lit his tenth Lucky Strike of the morning. The Dovekey volunteer ambulance was pulled onto the twenty-foot-wide dock; Maggie and Asa Fleck, the eager middle-aged married couple manning the rescue vehicle, stood beside it, shifting from one foot to the other in the damp chill. They had bought matching international orange broadcloth jumpsuits that, though natty, were not warm enough for so early in the season. In another month, they would be too hot, but still fetching, the doctor was sure.

Their fidgeting became more agitated as Ginny Philbrick's police boat neared its mooring.

"Think we'll need the cardiac equipment, Doc?" Asa asked with a serious frown.

"We're fully qualified to operate it," Maggie added hopefully.

Ryan stubbed out his cigarette and shook his head. "Just glove up, and shake out a body bag. If Al could have been resuscitated, we would have been notified."

"Al?" Maggie twisted her neck around as would a high-strung hamster. "Al who?"

"You know who they pulled up?" Asa nudged. "Al Spizzirri? Al Prather? Al Who?"

The doctor had a perverse urge to make the Odd Couple chew on their own curiosity for a while, but wasn't convinced enough of their professionalism in the face of a waterlogged corpse to indulge his impish bent.

"Al Jenness," he said.

"Al *Jenness?*" the makeshift Greek chorus chirruped in unison. "Selectman Jenness?" they tolled as one.

"Ayuh," Ryan nodded, lighting another unfiltered Lucky as Ginny Philbrick tied up.

"Ah-ha," Maggie intoned sagely to her husband. "I told you. Didn't I tell you?" Asa sighed in affirmation. "It wasn't an accident, was it, Doc? It was"—she lowered her voice to a whisper—"a mob hit, wasn't it?"

Ryan was taken aback by the confidence expressed in the bizarre question.

"Not so's you'd notice," he muttered, and waved wearily to Ginny, who was trudging surefootedly up the bobbing gangplank.

"Ginny!" Maggie Fleck shouted into Ryan's previously good ear, and ran past him to the chief of police. "Ginny! Is it true? Was Al Jenness *murdered* by the Cosa Nostra?" She pronounced it in the proper New England fashion, "coser nostrer."

Ryan silently reminded himself to recommend that the director of the volunteer fire department start running psychological checks on those who signed on for ambulance duty. Of course, *someone* had to enjoy hermetically sealing the dead. It just left a bad taste in the old man's mouth that there were couples walking around his town who did it in lieu of, say, watching television or having rare, uninspired sex.

"Why," Ginny asked, "would the mob knock off the local politician who was *backing* legalized gambling and prostitution, Maggie?"

"I don't know," Maggie answered, frowning with neuron-scorching concentration. Her face relaxed in wonderment at her own powers of deduction. "To throw us off the trail!"

Ginny started to miss New York, a town that simply didn't give a shit and so was often easier to manage.

"Is that the *Curmudgeon* pulling in with the Coasties?" Asa Fleck asked breathlessly, elbowing his wife with a knowledgeable look. "It *is,*" he confirmed without assistance. "It'd figure, wouldn't it?"

"What would figure, Asa?" Ginny asked. Why had she missed this hometown enough to give up a rent-stabilized apartment on the Upper West Side, she wondered, searching her pockets for an ibuprofen to dry-swallow.

"Well, that Frank Will would be in this somehow," Maggie answered for her husband. "You were at the Town Meeting last night, same as us. Al Jenness and Frank Will were going at it hammer and tongs. Asa even said to me that he had no intention of getting between those two old bulls once they got their het up. Looks like the boys took their disagreement outside after all." The woman's head bobbed rapidly up and down in vigorous agreement with herself. "Shoulda figured. Just a matter of time till Frank got violent. Everybody's always said so, haven't you, Asa?"

Ginny ambled away from the water and toward the omniscient Asa. "You always say that, Asa?" She was taller than he by several inches and had to stoop to look into his spider-veined face.

"Well, holy gawd, Gin," Asa protested, pulling out of striking distance, just in case, "not a person alive in Dovekey hadn't said the same thing. Prob'ly the dead ones, too." Impervious to such subtleties as irony, Asa backed farther away and looked to his wife for backup. None was forthcoming.

"Listen to me, Asa." Ginny put a strong arm around his shoulder. "What we got here is an ongoing investigation. The last thing I need is a duck shoot, y'hear?" Asa nodded somberly. "Now, the only reason you and Maggie are here at all is because the county coroner position is currently being held by some asswipe political appointee in Exeter, and the condition of Jenness's body is not conducive to the backseat of his BMW three-twenty-five-i-e. You following me?" Asa's balding head bowed twice in acknowledgment. "Now, we don't know for a *fact* that Al's death was intentional. So if I wander into the Breakfast 'n' Beans tomorrow morning for my coffee and hear anybody say anything close to the word 'homicide,' I'm going to be all over your ass like eczema." Over her shoulder, Ginny added, "Y'hear me, Maggie?"

"Oh, I hear you, Ginny," Maggie enunciated with great dignity. "Did you learn to be so uppity in New York City, or have you always been so wicked suspicious?"

Ginny ignored the feeble jab and pointed to Asa. "Help the guys tie up, will you? Maggie, hand me the body bag."

Elizabeth, guiltily relieved to be out and away from the water that had swallowed and then spat up Al Jenness, preceded the men off the boats and onto the dock. She refused Ryan's offer of a sedative before she considered spending the balance of the day with her father—without benefit of medication—and allowed the physician past her, down the gangplank, and onto the Coast Guard cruiser. Ryan was impressed by Elizabeth's newfound self-control, just as he had been previously impressed by her lack of it.

Ginny tossed the large black plastic bag off the end of the dock and onto the military deck. Frank caught the heavy-gauge sheeting with a quick grab of one hand and disappeared belowdeck.

"Okay, volunteers," Ginny ordered Asa and Maggie, "go on board and earn your place in heaven. I'll be earning mine by informing the new widow. Me." Ginny pointed to her chest. "Not anybody else. And remember what I said about the B 'n' B tomorrow!"

Tweedledum & Tweedledee trundled off dutifully, rolling their eyes at each other.

"Was it?" Elizabeth asked.

"What?" Ginny answered, patting her jacket pocket and pulling out a pack of cigarettes.

"Murder," Elizabeth said, against her better judgment.

"What do you think?" Ginny found her lighter, bent away from the wind, and lit up. Her cropped hair barely moved in the gusts from offshore.

"What do *I* think?" Elizabeth took a drag off Ginny's cigarette and handed it back with a grimace. She'd forgotten she had quit to spite her father more than a year ago. He had quit first, but wanted at least one member of the family to continue flying in the face of the Surgeon General's best advice. So, of course, Elizabeth had thrown away a full carton when she did not yet want to. "This is not therapy, Gin. You're the pro here. Was it or was it not murder?"

"Golly, Biz, that's a toughie." Ginny blew a blast of smoke. "Let's see. A real estate agent and duly elected government official is found seven miles out to sea with his head rammed into the three-inch opening of a lobster trap the night after a political free-for-all. I don't know." She handed her friend the cigarette. *"Could* have been an accidental drowning."

Elizabeth took a second, much better-tasting drag off the cigarette, exhaled, and handed it back. "I hate it when you talk to me like that. You sound just like my father."

"I always was his favorite," Ginny answered, knowing it was almost true. Wednesday-night poker with Frank's buddies had been a part of her and Elizabeth's upbringing ever since Frank had taught them to count cards. That had been when the two girls were around eleven. Elizabeth, ever the rebel, had always contended it was somehow cheating.

"So it *was* murder."

"Or one hell of an inventive way to commit suicide," Ginny commented, crushing her cigarette on the wormy boards of the dock.

Elizabeth looked at the smashed tube of tobacco longingly.

FOUR

BEN RYAN'S WIFE had canceled his morning hospital rounds and office appointments, and made a larger than usual pot of coffee. She had set everything up in a corner of the original 1940s-style surgery before she went to her twice-a-week league at the Bowl-O-Rama on Lafayette Road.

Ginny took a swig of black coffee from the clunky off-white ceramic Navy mug and lined up her shot. The Polaroid flashed and whirred on the last negative in the film pack. Ten would have to do. Ginny didn't think the Widow Jenness would be wanting copies for the corporate Christmas cards, anyway.

"So?" she asked the doctor.

Ryan lit a cigarette, handed it to her, and lit another for himself. The body was already raising a stink, and the acrid smoke helped cover it.

"He's dead," Ryan pronounced.

"Caught that part, Dr. Ryan. But since Ruth Jenness just may ask, you got any ideas of how it happened?"

"Nope."

Ginny exhaled in exasperation. "Okay. Any idea how it *didn't* happen?"

"Wasn't drowning."

"How do you know?"

"Can't be sure," Ryan answered, and flicked cigarette ash into an ancient petri dish. "Have to do a full autopsy, but Al doesn't *look* like he drowned. Know what I mean?"

Ginny knew.

The chief of police of any waterfront community sees too many drownings. There is a signature about the panic that is imprinted on the face after that first—and last—desperate gulp for oxygen that doesn't get washed off. Al Jenness didn't have that look.

Nor did the lobster pot.

Every lobsterman constructs his own pots, from woodwork to the knitted heads that trap and hold the catch. Al was encased in one of Frank Will's endeavors, not notable for its fine craftsmanship. Surely a reasonably healthy male in his mid-fifties would have succeeded in ripping away one or two of Frank's shoddy slats.

The pot was as pristine as it had ever been.

"Could he have been knocked unconscious before his head was stuck in there?" Ginny asked.

"Maybe. But it's damned hard to knock a man out. Harder than you'd believe if you watch television. Even harder to keep a person knocked out for more than a second or two." Ryan examined the netting around the corpse's neck. "See here? The knitting was slit to get the head in and then resecured with another piece of twine. That takes time."

Ginny nodded. "That water's cold enough to wake the dead on impact, too."

Ryan glanced at the corpse out of the corner of one eye. "Apparently not." He unlaced the dead man's shoes, but bloating made it impossible to remove them. "Gonna have to cut these off. Want to hand me those surgical shears, Ginny?"

"How long is this going to take, Doc?" Ginny asked, bringing over a tray of instruments.

"Longer than it ought," Ryan answered, holding up his hands for inspection. "Arthritis," he offered in explanation. "Don't tell me you have something more entertaining scheduled for this morning?"

"Gotta give Ruth Jenness the bad news before the Dovekey Beach communications network gets to her. Thought I'd better go talk to Frank and Biz right after. Might as well get it over with."

"Not possible to talk to Frank," Ryan mumbled as he cut away Al Jenness's sodden clothing: expensive, designer, indulgent for an umpteenth-generation Yankee. *Oh, well, life is short.* The lobsters had eaten away the flesh nearly an inch up and under the 100 percent pima cotton shirtsleeves. "Frank talks at *you.*"

"Don't I know it," Ginny responded, finishing off her coffee, "but a woman's got to do what a woman's got to do. You need me for anything?"

"Not till later. The state troopers are picking up the trap for labwork later this morning. I'm going to tape-record as I go along. You're going to have to transcribe. I'd have my wife do it, but she refuses ever since that cannibalism thing a few years ago in Seabrook."

"Sure," Ginny said at the door. "I don't exactly type, but I'll be happy to hunt and peck for you. Just make note of anything that seems at all strange."

"I guess that would be everything, wouldn't it?" Ryan clicked on the tiny tape recorder and went to work.

Ginny drove the powder-blue Ford along the old beach road. Cheap decals had been poorly applied to both front doors of the no-frills four-year-old car. From any distance, the only thing that gave the vehicle away as police transport was the removable blue bubble light stuck awkwardly just over the driver's door.

There was another car just like it, garaged until tourist season, when Mr. Elwell—otherwise known as the gym teacher from Dovekey Beach Junior High—picked up the "to protect and serve" slack. Ginny would never perform any high-speed maneuvers in the old tanker, but even Frank Will had to admit, the town had gotten one hell of a deal on the cars from the Air Force when the feds had closed down Pease Air Force Base.

Ginny's mind raced along with the fields of salt marsh hay on her right. Route 1-A would be impossible in another month when the sightseers arrived en masse. Unfortunately, the lack of deadly traffic gave Ginny a shorter trip and less time to think that morning.

What was Al Jenness doing dead in one of Frank Will's pots?

And there was no doubt that it was Frank's pot. Ginny had meticulously checked the riggings on the *Curmudgeon*. The buoy was undeniably Frank's own, and there was no missing the "F.W." burned into the side slat of the pot. The whole thing stank like a rotting salt marsh at low tide.

It wouldn't make any sense for Frank to pull up a body in front of his own daughter, with everything but a sign attached saying, "MINE, MINE, MINE."

Unless, of course, Frank was being incredibly devious. And deviousness was not an unspoken accusation from every citizen of the town at one time or another. Frank Will was as amusing as a good wine, but much less to everyone's taste. In fact, a town story was still circulating about the day Father Labas—the summer Catholic priest—clocked Frank with a chair during a heated theological discussion over steak and eggs at the Breakfast 'n' Beans.

Sooner than she would have liked, Ginny found herself throwing the car into park in the space next to Ruth Jenness's black Lincoln Town Car. Jenness Realty's faux beach cottage of weathered cedar shakes stood just past the Town Common, across from the junior high school and next to Foye's Pharmacy. The delft-blue window boxes that matched the decorative shutters were filled with pine boughs until warmer weather permitted the planting of red and white geraniums. Ruth was very fussy about neatness.

The chief of police found herself craving a cherry Coke.

Tucked in the rear of the Foyes' white Victorian pharmacy (white was the only color for buildings in the center of the village) stood the last of the soda fountains, replete with polished mahogany bar, brass fixtures, and sparkling white ceramic knobs. Ginny glanced at the bay window of Jenness Realty next door, then took a deep breath and blew it out noisily. No point in thinking this over; Ruth had to be told. It didn't matter whether Ruth was sitting at a neat desk in her obsessively tidy office or over a cup of coffee at home. Ginny just wished it could happen without her.

A motion detector in the jamb of the office door sounded an electronic *bong, bong* to announce Ginny's entrance. Ruth Jenness was standing at a tall filing cabinet behind Al's desk, her perfectly coiffed head bent over an open drawer.

"Be right with you," Ruth said without turning around. She was dressed in a handsome teal suit, exquisitely tailored to her tall, slim figure. Ginny was relieved to see that the office was still empty. The last thing she wanted was an audience.

"It's just me, Ruth. Ginny."

"Help yourself to some coffee, Ginny. I think I've just about figured out Al's filing system here, so don't distract me by reporting that kids are smoking dope in the old Sylvester place again. A couple from Worcester put a deposit on it yesterday, so it's not my headache anymore. Ah-ha!" Ruth pulled a listing sheet out of a manila folder. "I knew I'd find it eventually." She detached a small piece of notepaper from the larger printed page and examined it carefully, running her tongue across her top teeth as she read.

Ginny stood frozen eighteen inches inside the door. She wanted to go to the other woman and ease into what she had to say. Actually, she simply wanted Ruth to guess what Ginny had come to tell her. Most of the time the loved ones did just that, guessed the worst, while Ginny stood, wooden with empathy, gagged with a sense of helplessness.

So there she hovered, trying to mouth the proper words and wanting a damned cherry Coke at nine-forty in the morning the way a junkie craves heroin.

"The Sylvester place is fine, Ruth." Couldn't Ruth see that Ginny had something terrible to say? What was wrong with her? How could any woman be that preoccupied? Ruth's attention was directed in its entirety to one three-by-five scrap of paper. As though catching herself doing something antisocial, Ruth folded the paper in half and transferred it to her left hand.

"Well, thank God for that," she said, pouring herself a cup of coffee and carrying it to her desk near the office entrance. "Get yourself a cup. Don't tell me you're finally in the market to buy yourself a place. This is the time, you know. Interest rates will never be lower." Still standing, she rearranged her desktop so that the brochures, contracts, and name plate were precisely parallel or perpendicular to one another.

Ginny tried to force herself to walk to Ruth's desk, to give the woman one more hint. Instead, she asked, "Is Betty coming in this morning?"

"Already late. You know, I think I have just the thing for you. Big old place, needs some fixing up, but you've always been handy. Has an outbuilding with insulation that could be converted easily into a studio for Sandy. She's always complaining that you two don't have the room for her to make any really big sculptures. This would do the trick nicely, I think."

Ruth's nattering became increasingly painful to the still immobile Ginny. Every word drove home how poorly she was handling the situation. It reminded her of swimming lessons on early-summer mornings when she and Elizabeth were children. The water in the harbor never rose over fifty degrees and the bottom was a slippery thick ooze that squeezed its way through toes and up to the ankle. The only way to get the lesson over was to jump immediately (without thinking, if possible) from the mushy bank and try not to scream.

Elizabeth always screamed and bitched to the high heavens.

Elizabeth would also know what to say to Ruth Jenness to get this lesson started and over with.

"I'm here about Al, Ruth. There's been an accident."

"Al? What kind of accident?" Ruth finally looked up to see the expression on Ginny's face. But she did not put down her cup of coffee. "How badly is he hurt?"

"It's bad, Ruth." Ginny could not force herself to finish, and that Ruth could not miss.

"He's dead?" The Royal Doulton "Old English Roses" bone china mug was placed carefully on a Dovekey Beach souvenir lobster coaster to the left of Ruth's blotter.

Ginny nodded but still could not bring herself to go to Ruth's side. "It happened sometime last night, Ruth."

"Well." Ruth exhaled, sinking heavily into the oak captain's chair behind her matching desk, yet still retaining her rigid posture. As an expression of her profound shock, she dropped the folded paper from her left hand next to the coffee mug. It opened exposing handwriting in black felt-tip. Masculine. Al Jenness reaching from the grave. "That explains that."

Too wretched to face Ruth's grief, Ginny focused on the fragment of stationery. Lots of numbers, no sentences, but one word: "Liz."

"What, Ruth?"

"Why the old bastard didn't come home last night."

Ginny pulled into the gravel parking lot of the Elizabeth Will Gallery, clutching the numbers she had copied from the paper Ruth Jenness had dropped when she heard the news about her husband. She parked next to Frank's ancient red pickup truck, easily identified by the body putty Frank smeared over the truly massive rust holes to get the truck through state vehicle inspection without ever bothering to paint over the patches. Elizabeth was constantly begging him to park up the driveway at the old Cape Cod house they shared, but Frank refused. He said the truck lent "local color," as did the traps he mended in the raised flower beds his daughter struggled to maintain. Elizabeth's white 1964 MGB was in its proper place behind the gallery, next to the sagging outbuilding that had once been a small barn. Both the building and the car were in desperate need of repairs.

Ginny tucked the copy of Al's final, cryptic message into her jacket pocket. "Liz: 176512398080." A deed registration number? It was time for Biz to move out of the family homestead, that was for sure, but first things first.

The gallery wasn't open for the season yet, but the parking spaces were "colorfully" littered with scrap lumber and plastic bait buckets. Elizabeth's sister, Avis Donigian, had parked her Yuppie Jeep along the shoulder of the road, just behind Jesse Kneeland's silver extended-cab truck. If she hadn't known better, Ginny would have thought it was a party—for a bunch of people with nothing in common whatsoever.

Avis greeted the police chief at the door just as though it were a party. She was darker than her sister. Two years younger. Shorter and less rangy. Funnier, too, though that had not always been so.

"Hey, Gin," Avis said, "I thought you'd get here sooner or later." She proffered a plate of what appeared to be neatly cut cubes of compost. "Have a granola bar. They're still warm."

"Hey, Moof." Ginny lifted a warm rectangle from the ironstone plate and examined it. "I'd heard you'd gone upscale and reactionary, but this"—she returned the granola suspiciously to its position and wiped her hand on her pants leg—"is too much."

"Moof?" Jesse repeated from where he sat slumped in the gallery proper. Avis and Ginny ignored him. The nickname was residue from a long-ago childhood joke about a cow with a congenital palate disfigurement. Jesse knew the story, though he had forgotten. It would return to him naturally in less time than it would take to remind him.

"How about some decaf, then?" Avis asked, going to the coffee machine on the long framing table at the rear of the large room. Elizabeth stood at the table slopping water on a large piece of watercolor paper neatly taped down on four sides.

"Coffee would be better," Ginny answered dourly. She poured from Frank's Army-issue thermos into a personalized hand-thrown pig mug, which she pulled from a peg on the wall. Elizabeth continued to work with manic concentration. She was obviously doing her iron maiden routine. The I-can-deal-with-this-and-be-productive-at-the-same-time thing she specialized in. Sometimes she even succeeded.

Jesse lit a hand-rolled cigarette; the smoke rose vibrantly white in the filtered sunlight. Avis efficiently positioned a cobalt-blue pottery bowl on his knee to catch ashes and opened the door for ventilation.

Ginny did not interrupt Elizabeth's flow of affected busywork.

"Gotta ask questions, right?" Elizabeth asked, still bent over the soggy watercolor paper. She studied her palette as though it could speak. "I have to work, if that's okay." The truth was she needed several things to do at the same time. If she could have knitted an afghan and put together a jigsaw puzzle simultaneously, she would have. It was yet another aberrant family trait.

"Fine," Ginny answered as Elizabeth moistened each well of the metal paint tray, one at a time, careful not to let the pigments pollute one another. Ginny watched in fascination as Elizabeth dropped a one-inch brush full of a dark, glowering gray-blue onto the upper right and lower left corners of the saturated paper. The color immediately started to swell and crawl along the wet buckles of the surface, as though it had a life of its own. Elizabeth dipped a tapered brush slightly smaller than the first into the clean water to her right, allowed droplets to fall onto the darkest spots of pigment, drew the bristles lightly over a paper towel to dry them, and then dragged the brush through the still-growing explosion of color on the sheet to create swirls that began to collide from the top of the page to the bottom. When the color was about to meet at the center, she caught the cascades with a deft blot of tissue.

How does she do that? Ginny wondered.

Amazing how that works, Elizabeth marveled and sat back on her stool. Sky and water, as easy as that. Add cattails—or a birch tree—or a line of land in the distance, and *Voilà!* Instant creativity. And once again, art miraculously imitates life. Supplement with a spray of seagulls, and *Voilà!* An income springs from a dry bag of tricks. She was suddenly very tired.

"Where's your dad?" Ginny asked either Avis or Elizabeth; it didn't matter who answered.

"Up at the house," the two sisters responded in unison, the way they often did. Elizabeth took over the lead, as was her duty as the elder. "He's making a lobster stew."

"Ah," Ginny said.

In times of trouble, Frank always made a lobster stew. The day the old family dog died, when Elizabeth was fourteen, Frank spent eleven hours making the perfect lobster stew while Sal, his wife, buried the dog and comforted her daughters. No one ate that stew; it sat in the freezer for years, until Sal brought home a new puppy and threw the stew out for the raccoons.

He made a lobster stew the day New Hampshire elected a Democrat governor and Frank announced his intention to move the family to New Zealand. Everyone ate that stew before going to bed to forget the whole business.

He made the best stew ever on the day Elizabeth graduated from college and Sal packed up bag and baggage to move to Boston to begin her sidetracked career as a romance novelist in some well-deserved peace and quiet, away from a gene pool in which she was not very well represented.

The newest dog ate that batch of stew and passed copious amounts of gas for days.

These days the Will family was on its third cocker spaniel. And Frank was at the stove again.

"Better bring your money and your appetite tonight," Elizabeth advised Ginny. "The old man must have taken thirty lobsters up to the house. My guess is, this is going to be the mother of all chowders."

It took Ginny a moment to make the connection. It was Wednesday: poker night with Frank and Biz.

"Sorry, Biz," Ginny answered.

"Well," Avis interjected from the front door, "I'm sure as hell not going to eat it all. Do you have any idea how much cholesterol there is in a bowl of that stuff? Might as well shoot up chocolate éclairs intravenously."

"Oh, no," Elizabeth muttered, shaking her head.

"That was a *joke*, Biz," Avis defended herself. "What happened to your sense of humor?"

"I lost it the minute I stopped being an only child." Elizabeth turned her attention back to Ginny. "You're not coming over tonight, is that it?"

Ginny nodded. "Afraid not."

"I can't *believe* you, Philbrick," Elizabeth said. Her jaw set in the way Avis recognized as dangerous. Elizabeth's jaw had clenched that way many years ago when Avis had "accidentally" poured four liters of Diet Pepsi into her piano.

"Okay"—Avis jumped in—"I'll come over for poker tonight. We'll play three-handed. No big deal. A gallon or two of Dad's lobster stew probably won't kill me. Not immediately." She glanced from Ginny to her sister. The jaw still looked that scary way she remembered from the time before Elizabeth decided to stop having a "strong personality." Avis rambled on. "The vet warned us: no more lobster for the dog; and you know how Dad gets when they die. It's a vicious cycle. Death, stew, more death, more stew."

"Shut up, Moof," Elizabeth ordered. "Ginny is telling us that she can't come over tonight because Dad is a suspect in Al Jenness's murder. That *is* what you're saying, isn't it, Gin?"

"What?" the all-but-forgotten Jesse asked through his fog of introspection in the corner.

"That's what I was saying," agreed Ginny without apology. "Can't do it, Biz. Wouldn't be proper."

Jesse reared up as though he'd been shot and cursed, "Mary on a bicycle, you can't be serious, Ginny."

"I am," she answered, miserable and a little angry at having to explain herself.

"She is," confirmed Elizabeth, similarly annoyed with the generally benign Jesse.

The struggle to construct a sentence or two of argument played out on Jesse Kneeland's kind face. The hovering cloud of disagreement among the three women evaporated in that instant. Ginny was right, of course, and they all three knew it. It was nothing personal.

Grabbing on to the first and most obvious thing that occurred to him, Jesse blurted, "Proper! Proper. I sure, by-jeezus, never would have expected to hear that word from you, Ginny Philbrick."

Color that showed anger, not embarrassment, rushed up from Ginny's neck and suffused her cheeks as she turned to face Jesse. Fortunately for him, Elizabeth's mouth was faster than her friend's.

"Bag it, Jess," Elizabeth warned.

"Well, all I can say is, she's got one hell of a nerve," Jesse blundered on, "to talk about"—he searched for an alternative word and failed—"*proper.*"

34

It wasn't as though Ginny hadn't been subjected to such accusations before. It was just that they'd never come from the innocuous, lumbering Jesse. Ginny was hanging on to her professional composure by her short, neat fingernails. Avis was clearly stumped for a reaction that she could reconcile with her finely tuned earth mother persona. Silence banged from wall to wall in the gallery.

In the clanging quiet, Elizabeth's joints unlocked. She stood, grasped the glass of brush-cleaning water from the desk, and flung the murky contents full force into Jesse's red, shocked face.

"You," she ordered him, "take your pulsating testosterone and raging homophobia out of my gallery before I say something you might *understand*. Understand?"

Clearly Jesse did not. Dirty water dripped from his forehead. He stood like a muddy puppy, ready for another inevitable swat with a rolled-up newspaper. Ginny took the glass from Elizabeth's clenched hand.

"It's okay, Biz," Ginny said with a control she wouldn't have bothered to muster had Elizabeth retained her own. "Jesse's upset. We're *all* upset." She turned to the flustered Jesse. "I'm not accusing Frank of anything, Jess. But I am the chief of police hereabouts, and I don't want the populace to go around screaming favoritism. I am going to do my job according to the book—and I would appreciate it if you would support me in this."

Jesse looked from Ginny to Elizabeth, whose fury still bordered on the murderous. It had taken a while, but the big man was ashamed of himself.

Just about anyone in the county who cared, and that would be everyone, knew that Ginny was a lesbian. Jesse supposed everyone had known it all the way back to Dovekey Beach Junior High School, though Ginny had always been too well liked to make it fodder for locker room discussion. He also knew that her "persuasion" didn't matter a damn. Not to him. Not then or now. He wanted to crawl under a rock, could he have lifted one large enough, and it showed.

"I didn't mean it, Gin," he mumbled.

Elizabeth pushed past Avis, who had positioned herself between her sister and the object of her sister's wrath. It was not so much bravery as it was the force of thirty years' habit. Avis often referred to herself as the soft, squishy white Oreo center between Frank's and Elizabeth's chocolate-cookie rages.

"Then why the *hell* did you say it?" Elizabeth demanded.

"Sit *down,* Biz," Ginny ordered. "We have got a shitload of trouble as it is, and I don't want to have to book my best friend in the world for assault. *Okay?* I am *busy.*"

As if to prove her point, a van marked with the logo of the Eternal Sea Group tore into the gallery parking lot amid a spray of gravel.

Before the dust had settled, they heard the furious slamming of the van door. A large, enraged man covered the distance to the gallery entrance in six long strides.

Elizabeth had hoped Frank would be tied up with his stew for a while longer.

The unforeseeable kept happening.

The afternoon was looking down.

FIVE

"BREAK OUT THE granola bars, Avis," Elizabeth muttered. "We have company." Next she solemnly asked Ginny, "Got another gun?"

Ginny smiled. "Now that the famous Liz Will temper has resurfaced, I think the public is better off with you unarmed." She was only half kidding. All the Wills were known for their short fuses, no matter how much Elizabeth damped hers down.

The night before, while the infamous Town Meeting slugfest had been going down, Ginny had been called away to a domestic dispute. Roland and Terri Ouimet were embroiled in their weekly custody battle over the statue of the Virgin Mary perched in the center of a sky-blue claw-footed bathtub upended on their front lawn. Ginny's assistance had been required primarily to safeguard the spindly Rollie, who had chained himself to his precious "Mary on the half-shell," from his aesthetically inclined wife and her trusty hedge clippers. But Ginny's roommate, Sandy, stayed at the equally entertaining Town Meeting and reported on it later, over a glass of decent red wine. Every cop—whether in New York or New Hampshire—has her informants.

Al Jenness had been magnificent. Everyone on his side of the dispute said so. But what was worth the price of admission was watching Big Frank Will unnaturally aligned with the kind of do-gooder organization that most gave him gas: namely, the Eternal Sea Group.

Frank did not approve of organized anything. But it had been his daughter Elizabeth who had been moved to inquire of the director of ESG how he could possibly conduct his research on microscopic animals with his head and equipment up his ass. They had stood nose to nose, naturally. If Elizabeth had stood an inch further away, her snipe might have missed shotgunning pellets of contempt all over her target.

Ginny and Sandy had laughed themselves silly over the dissection of their respective evenings. Now, with Al Jenness being laid open by Doc Ryan's hands rather than Frank Will's wit, it didn't seem so funny. Ginny made a mental note to question Sandy more carefully about the particulars of the Town Meeting as soon as she got home. At that moment, however, Ginny's attention was better directed toward the present.

The driver of the Eternal Sea Group van came through the door of the gallery as though he could just as easily have come through the wall. He was in his early forties, six feet tall, very dark brown hair (burnt sienna, Elizabeth would have said on a more forgiving day) worn a bit too long so that it curled loosely about his ears, hazel eyes that leaned toward dark green, and a construction worker's stubble and demeanor, which belied his Ph.D. in marine botany.

Elizabeth and Avis immediately recognized him from the night before. He had been standing next to their father, looking for all the world like Frank's long-lost son; he was the only man present capable of projecting more arrogant smugness. Even Al Jenness had taken a reflexive step backward, away from Elizabeth, when the shouting began. This Dr. Charles MacKay, director of ESG, took up a lot of room wherever he stood. Even nose to nose with a pugnacious Elizabeth Will.

And where he stood on the question of legalized prostitution and gambling was in direct opposition to Al Jenness and the Will sisters.

Frank had pegged MacKay as a bleeding-heart plankton-hugger, and said so, and said so, and said so. But that did not stop him from supporting the scientist at the Town Meeting against his own children.

It was an uneasy alliance at best. Frank did not want his fishing territory fouled; MacKay did not want his seaweed mucked. At least that was what MacKay said. Frank refused to believe that there could be a lofty principle involved in the preservation of slimy sea vegetation beyond that of biodegradable sushi wrapping.

MacKay was damned secretive, Frank opined.

And if the townsfolk had heard it once, they'd heard it a thousand times. So it was with morbid fascination that they watched the unlikely duo of Frank Will and Charles MacKay face off against Elizabeth, Avis, and Al.

Better than *Dallas,* several said on the way home after the hearing. More peculiar than *Northern Exposure,* a few others commented. Sandy thought it was funnier than *Cheers.*

No one was laughing now.

"What the hell are you doing here, Philbrick?" MacKay bellowed. "While you gaze at fine art or whatever the hell this is, there are two Coast Guard cruisers farting around my docking area churning up enough foam for a bubble bath, throwing around lobster pots, and trailing an oil slick thick enough to walk on to the mainland." MacKay's agitation had already raised a sweat; he removed his parka and dropped it on the floor as he walked up into Ginny's face. "There are a couple dozen private and commercial boats jamming what little harbor area we have, taking pictures like goddamn Japanese tourists and frightening the hell out of the fish.

Nobody answers the phone or the radio at the station. I've been cruising around the village for an hour trying to spot your car. What is the *matter* with you?"

Elizabeth picked up the discarded parka and handed it to MacKay. "That's 'Goddess of Protection, Sir' to you, buddy." Avis guffawed before she could catch herself. MacKay observed Elizabeth as though she were a rare but not especially interesting specimen on which he had prepared a slide during college.

"Okay, okay." Ginny called a halt. "Knock it off, you guys. Liz, put a granola bar in it and settle down. MacKay, for your information the Coasties are pulling pots on my order. They should be through by now."

"Well, isn't that a relief to the ecosystem," MacKay spat. "I've been complaining about a breach of security on Piscatawk for months now, and you're telling me that the first sign of government activity I see is to haul traps for the locals?"

"I'd can the hostility if I were you, Dr. MacKay. You're the one who won't give me authorization to check out that little pimple on the ass of the Atlantic out there." Ginny honed in. "And as for however many boatloads of sightseers there are bobbing around God's little half-acre, they have as much right to the water—if not the island—as you do. And"—she cut him off mid–mouth flap—"if you ever spoke to any of the natives like real people, you'd know that Al Jenness was pulled up dead fifty yards from your dock just after dawn this morning. *That's* what is going on to disturb your tight-assed intellectual tranquility."

MacKay took a short beat. "Al Jenness, the selectman, is dead?" he asked.

"Murdered," Elizabeth elaborated, hoping to blanch the healthy tan from his handsome face and bow some of the arrogance in his shoulders.

"My God," MacKay whispered.

40

"God rest his soul," offered Jesse.

"Pray for all of us," Elizabeth said, nudging Ginny and pointing to the back window. "Here comes my father. And he's carrying something."

SIX

FRANK WAS INSIDE the gallery door and in Charles MacKay's face while the others were still making up their minds whether it would be better to intervene or just watch the inevitable unfold.

Sunlight made the metal in Frank's right hand gleam, casting jittering reflections below MacKay's square jaw. Avis couldn't help noticing the attractive cleft in that jaw and a small scar showing through the two-day growth of beard—and the way her sister emphatically did not notice them.

Neither of the two big men paid attention to anyone else or gave an inch of territory.

"Here, MacKay," Frank ordered, aggressively raising the metal in his hand. "Taste this."

MacKay took the greasy tablespoon from Frank, gave him a suspicious look, and swallowed with a defiant flourish.

No one broke the silence. MacKay dangled the empty spoon disdainfully from his left hand.

"It's cold, Will. The butter's all congealed on the top."

"I am aware of that, MacKay," Frank harrumphed, grabbing the spoon back. "It's chilly out; I had to walk it down a hundred yards from the kitchen. Of course it's cold." He rearranged his face into a pseudo-conciliatory expression. "That's physics, Mr. Wizard. All I want to hear from you is what's missing."

MacKay shifted his feet to mirror Frank's belligerent posture. "Leeks."

"Leeks! Leeks? Leeks don't live in lobster stew. What kind of Philistine are you, anyway?"

"Philistine? Philistine?"

The spoon made a dull thunk as it hit the gallery floor. Veins stood out on the necks of the marine botanist and the lobsterman. Elizabeth went back to her painting; Avis downed half a granola bar in one bite. Jesse looked hurt that Frank had offered the tasting job to another man; Ginny rubbed her temples to try to collect herself.

There were times she missed the peace and quiet of New York City, where the sheer foreignness of the populace helped her maintain her objectivity without effort. Knife fights over gang turf seemed moronic beyond belief, yet somehow Ginny could relate easily to the prospect of bloodshed over lobster seasoning. Rolling her eyes at her own idiocy, she marched to a position between the men, mildly surprised that Elizabeth was not in the thick of the mess as well.

"Frank, give me that right now," she commanded, removing the Tupperware container from his left hand and raising it to her mouth. She spat a lump of hardened butter back into the bowl before returning it to Frank. "You forgot the Lawrey's Seasoned Salt, Frank."

"Right!" Frank agreed and then turned back into MacKay's personal space. "Leeks, indeed."

"It's *your* heart." MacKay shrugged. "Monosodium glutamate, animal fat. Go ahead and kill yourself, just don't take me with you."

"Who invited you?"

Ginny grimaced with frustration. MacKay and Frank simply had too much attitude for one small room. Or a large one, for that matter. She was going to have to divide and conquer, and figured that seven miles was probably about the minimal necessary distance.

"All right, boys, break it up. Frank, go to your room. I'll be back to check the stew later. Dr. MacKay, why don't you and I float back out to the isles and see what we can see out there, okay?"

"Thank you, Chief. I think that's an excellent idea," MacKay agreed. Elizabeth grunted loudly and disdainfully enough that no one missed it. "Your dinghy or mine?" MacKay further inquired with surprising puckishness.

"Oh, God," Elizabeth moaned in disgust.

"Let's go Dutch," Ginny said. "I'll meet you out there on the Piscatawk pier in an hour. And I'll be expecting the Cook's tour."

"My pleasure." MacKay nodded. Elizabeth looked up at that moment and caught his eye. He looked down at the watercolor on the table in front of her. "I'd like to see that when it's done. Rather interesting use of Payne's gray."

"Thanks," Elizabeth muttered to the big man's back, not flattered in the least. It was an absolutely *banal* use of the color. Nonetheless, she watched Charles MacKay drive away. "You know where to find me," she offered grimly to the empty space where he'd stood. She fancied it was still warm.

"Well," Frank said, breaking into everyone's thoughts, "the stew will be ready in about six hours. If you bring the kids, Avis, you'd better pick up some more oyster crackers."

"Gerald took the kids to see his folks, Dad. I told you. Two weeks."

"Terrific," Frank said. "More for me" were his last words as he headed out the door.

"Think it's genetic?" Avis asked her big sister.

"No doubt in my mind," Elizabeth answered and stood up to shake out her shoulders. This morning she would have thought she couldn't have gotten more tense. "Thank God for new advances in

DNA manipulation; otherwise I'd have a call in to Dr. Kevorkian."

Although Ginny wanted another cup of coffee and a chance to reconcile with the Will sisters, duty was not only calling, but shouting.

"Jesse, are you heading back out to the shoals?"

"Uh, ayuh. Thought I would. There're some ruins I wanted to look at again on one of the other islands. Smith's Isle. The littlest one," he explained eagerly. "Just my hobby. You know. Pots are all in and it's still early."

"Perfect," Ginny said, picking up her parka and tossing Jesse's into his lap. "I'd like a ride, if that's okay with you. We'll drag the town skiff along so you don't have to wait for me to finish—or vice versa."

Ginny knew better than to try to make schedules around Jesse's newest enthusiasm: history. The border dispute between Maine and New Hampshire over which state owned the Portsmouth Naval Shipyard had got Jesse started. And, like a boulder barreling down a hill, once Jesse got rolling his own momentum kept him moving right up the next incline. Whatever had convinced him that he would be able to discover conclusive evidence that the Granite State had the first colonial claim to the territory, when historians from opposing universities had been squabbling since the turn of the century, Ginny did not know. She just knew that Jesse was on one of his rolls. As Frank would say, "That's physics." She was just glad she would only have to make the one return trip from the shoals in the too-small and too-light police skiff. One round trip alone for the day was enough.

And after finally getting a close-up look at MacKay's inner sanctum, she would have the perfect excuse to stick her nose into another secret society for which she was responsible, without knowing much about them.

How long since anyone from town had been on Cap's Island? One hundred years at least since the resort hotel had been built by some religious group or another and thirty-some since it had been sold to Garrett Selby. Ginny begged her own pardon—the Reverend Garrett Selby and his Children of Deity. Even peculiar people deserved their titles.

The congregation stuck strictly to themselves. No proselytizing or socializing. Members trotted through town only long enough to wait for the tour ship or water taxis to pick them up and take them to the enclave, or to check out historical records at the Athenaeum in downtown Portsmouth. There was never any reported trouble traced to Cap's, and New Englanders' natural suspicion of outright displays of religion (let alone, God forbid, fervor) kept the island secluded in the extreme. But there were people out there. People who might have seen something the night before. People who just might be able to save Frank Will's recalcitrant butt.

She chided herself for being so jaded, but she didn't think bailing out Frank Will was top priority on Charles MacKay's to-do list for this decade. Or anyone else's, for that matter. In fact, she was a little afraid that Elizabeth was about ready to pull the gallows trap herself.

The prospect of a big bowl of lobster stew was beginning to appeal to Ginny, despite her high ethical standards. Further investigation might be necessary by dinnertime.

That was, of course, if the rest of the afternoon didn't ruin her appetite.

SEVEN

ELIZABETH WILL WAS crying. It would be hard to say who was more surprised: Elizabeth herself, or her sister. They were finally alone in the gallery, and Avis kicked herself for having thought it would be better that way.

Elizabeth's breathing hitched irregularly until she leaned over her watercolor table, bracing herself on rigid arms, lowered her golden-copper head, and sucked air into her lungs determinedly. That was how Avis knew for certain that Elizabeth was in deep, dark trouble. That's how she always knew.

What Avis *never* knew was exactly what to do about her sister's crying. She had not had a lot of experience comforting Elizabeth; it had never been her job. As the younger, her job had always been to be the crier, not the cryee; the sensitive rather than the sensible. Her hands felt like huge clammy hams hung at her wrists. She wanted so desperately to say exactly the right thing to comfort Elizabeth that her stomach retreated into a small leaden thing cowering at the bottom of her abdomen. But the perfect words would not come to her lips, nor could she muster a sisterly hug from her gangly arms. Cursing her outdated Puritan reserve, Avis did the only thing she knew how.

She started to cry, too.

Elizabeth looked up from her rhythmic breathing exercise. One tear fell sloppily down her cheek, landing in the center of the carefully executed watercolor sky. The salt in the tear sucked pigment into itself like a black hole consuming an unsuspecting star system.

"What the hell are you doing?"

"I am *not* crying," Avis defended herself. "Besides, you started it."

"Did not," Elizabeth denied feebly, taking a tissue for herself and another for Avis, who accepted it with haughty dignity. "I hate it when you cry with me."

"I'm not," Avis protested and blew her nose.

"I'm okay now."

"Are not."

"Am now."

Avis decided not to press. "Okay." Time marched on. "Beer?"

"I think we should."

"Me too." Avis ducked into the back room where Elizabeth did her picture framing and returned with two cans of Guinness stout. She popped one and handed it to Elizabeth. It was not state-of-the-art sisterly comfort, but it was the best she could do at that moment. She would ease into the important talk sideways and in her own good time.

Elizabeth took a long swallow, closed her eyes in contentment, and said, "These are Dad's, you know."

"What isn't?" Avis asked and took a pull at her can. "Makes them taste better."

"Always has."

"Don't suppose you want to talk about it," Avis said over the top of her can. "Finding Al's body, I mean." She backpedaled before her sister could figure out what she really meant: the question that had been running loops in the gerbil cage of Avis's mind for a couple of months.

"Don't suppose I do," Elizabeth answered calmly. Noticing Avis's crestfallen look, she added, "Probably will eventually, though." The sisters sat in comfortable silence and sipped.

"You think Dad's really a suspect?" Avis shifted gears, feeling guilty and disloyal.

"Don't you?"

"Who wouldn't suspect Dad?" Avis answered with resignation.

"But it's so damned pat. Dad and Al get in a huge fight—in public, no less—and the next morning Dad pulls up his own trap with Al's body hanging out of it." The sisters' eyes met. "Why do I worry, anyway? It almost guarantees that the police are going to look somewhere else for the murderer. Never heard of a murderer that stupid. Well, I don't know *anyone* that stupid."

Avis chucked her empty into a trash can across the room. "Three points," she awarded herself. "Neither do I."

The sisters sat quietly, thinking the same thought: that they couldn't come up with anyone dumb enough to implicate Frank without knowing Ginny would investigate elsewhere. But they could certainly think of someone Machiavellian enough to accuse himself and let the police double-think him out of it.

"He didn't, did he?" Avis asked softly.

"Dad?"

"Uh-huh."

"Nahh," Elizabeth tossed off, and then muttered something under her breath.

"What are we going to do?" Avis asked. "Play poker and eat ourselves sick?"

"Right. A gold star for our Miss Moof."

"But you don't really think . . ."

"I'm trying not to, Avis. I'm really trying."

Ben Ryan sat at the kitchen table, alternately rubbing the sore joints of his hands and throwing cold bits of buttered toast to his geriatric German shepherd, Howard. The dog was getting so old and slow that tidbits she could have caught in the air during her younger days now bounced off her nose and skittered across the red and black kitchen tiles—to be stepped on by bare feet the next morning. It was a major point of contention between Ben and his wife.

The autopsy on Al Jenness was finished and the tape of the doctor's comments sat on the table before him awaiting transcription. It had been a tough one.

They were all tough ones. Ryan was no pathologist. He had hated working on cadavers as a medical student, and he hated it more now. A small-town physician knows everyone for miles around, and there is a damned big difference between sawing into a lifeless stranger and dissecting a man you treated for hemorrhoids the week before.

Adding insult to injury, Ryan had quickly discovered that Selectman Jenness was going to have to be "done" again—probably in Concord. Ryan's expertise was only enough to support an obvious case of accidental death: mere paperwork. This was not one of those cases. The doctor shook his head wearily.

"Howard, old girl, on top of old-fashioned murder, we seem to have a logistical problem here." Ryan tossed a piece of toast, which bounced off Howard's nose and under the refrigerator. The dog searched the floor, baffled, until the doctor placed another snack directly in her mouth; this she swallowed without chewing as she looked at her master quizzically.

"Oh, it's murder all right." The doctor paused and reconsidered. "Well, there was no water in the lungs, so we know it wasn't drowning. There was a cerebral hemorrhage, certainly, but how many times did I warn that old fart to stop smoking and get some exercise?" Ryan leaned back in the kitchen chair and lit a cigarette.

"The injury to the head is consistent with a fall. Splinters from wood decking in the abrasion, you know. And the stroke probably brought on the heart attack that actually was the modus exodus.

"Now, I know that sounds like death by natural causes, old girl, but it was no act of God that wound Al's neck into that trap and sank him to the bottom of the Atlantic. Took some extra weight to ballast the body, too, what with that spare tire around Al's gut. Fat floats, you know, no matter how well you camouflage it in Italian silk suits. Anyway, the point I'm trying to make is that it surely wouldn't surprise the hell out of me to find out that Al's coronary was brought *on* by having his head Cinch-sacked, and that, old girl, is surer than shit murder. Technically, at least."

Edith Ryan closed the kitchen door behind her and dropped the leather bag that contained her three custom candlepin bowling balls into the dry sink. The color-coordinated Brunswick shoes were still tucked under her arm.

"Ben, how many times have I told you to stop talking to that dog. You got something to share, share it with me. Your patients will think you're touched."

Ryan smiled up at his wife. Her cheeks were flushed from her morning's exercise, and she looked damned fine in her new black spandex pants and oversized bowling shirt.

"I'm the only doctor in town. What are they going to do, take their myocardial infarctions elsewhere? Anyway, Howard's the only one who doesn't think I'm touched. That's why we get along so well."

"Stop feeding her all that junk and see how friendly she stays." Edith poured herself a cup of coffee and sat next to her husband at the table. She laid her hand companionably on his thigh. "So what's on your mind that you have to share it with an animal instead of your significant other?"

"Hard to say. There's something nagging away at me, but I can't quite shake it free."

"That's it?"

"Well, maybe one more thing. I just may have illegally sliced and diced Al Jenness." Howard let out a loud snore from beneath the table. "Those island boundaries slip around as much as Fred Astaire tapping in a cow patty. I don't know which jurisdiction the body was found in."

"*That's* your worry?" Edith asked. "Then ask Jesse Kneeland, or call the Athenaeum; either one will have the latest marine charts."

"Nah. That's not what's really bothering me. I don't *know* what's really bothering me."

"So stop worrying about jurisdictions."

"Well, I just hate breaking the law by accident."

Edith shook her head and smiled.

"You know, Ben, I love you more than a woman married this long has a right to, but I can't help but notice that sometimes you sound a lot like Frank Will. It scares me."

"Me too," Ryan agreed. "Me too."

Frank Will whistled a complicated sea jig to himself, surgical shears snapping in time with the music. To punctuate an especially gratifying passage, he tossed a carcass into one of two white plastic pails: lobster bodies to be taken out for the raccoons, shells for the garbage. Frank felt unapologetically terrific.

He sank a wooden spoon deep into the roiling five-gallon stockpot and came up with a steaming puddle of cream and lobster. He blew twice and tasted. One eyebrow shot up appreciatively.

"By George," Frank complimented himself, "I believe I've done it again." He lowered the spoon to a foot off the linoleum floor. "Tell me honestly, Petunia, how right I am," he instructed the overweight black cocker spaniel. Petunia lifted the lobster off the spoon and swallowed thoughtfully, then licked at the cream with less enthusiasm. "More seasoned salt?" Frank asked the dog.

Petunia sprawled across his slippered feet. "I thought so, too," he answered himself.

Yes, Frank Will felt better than he had in some time. *Life can get so by-dammit dull, and most of the time death isn't much better. But every now and again, a man gets lucky.*

Frank started to whistle the 1812 Overture as Petunia snored, oblivious to everything except dreams of lobster stew.

EIGHT

THE ISLES RANG with sound. Gulls and cormorants cawed and bleated as they rode wind currents down to the ocean, feet skittering over the surface, knife-point bills stabbing for shallow-swimming fish. Other birds bobbed quietly, like discarded Styrofoam cups in a giant puddle.

The morning's wind had died, transforming the sea's diamond-tipped chops into quartz-glass swells. Charles MacKay felt as though he could simply skate the final mile to the experimental station, the same way the birds skated the gusts of air. No wonder he had been having the most incredible dreams of flying lately. So many months spent living surrounded by ocean. Who wouldn't feel weightless? Unfettered by convention? What little time he now spent onshore was heavy and unsatisfying, as though gravity had twice the pull as when he was within his small world. MacKay's work was so real that mere life made him anxious.

The coastline continued to diminish at his back, further separating him from the eccentrics and quibblers on shore at Dovekey Beach. No matter that the buildings on Piscatawk were as severe and cold as condos by Khrushchev; after fifteen months of solitude they meant comfort and home to the reclusive Ph.D. Not that

MacKay enjoyed his near-hermit's existence; it worked out better for him, that was all. As his colleagues had often said, Charles MacKay was socially challenged. MacKay didn't mind.

He'd been called far worse.

He was agreeably surprised to see that the Coast Guard had gone back to Fort Constitution at Newcastle, leaving his island to its own devices. The gawkers had also left the area for whatever passed as their normal lives. Church bells rang loudly from nearby Cap's Island. MacKay wondered how many times a day people could benefit from religious services, anyway. Because the bells annoyed him, he wanted to believe that they also disturbed the bird life on surrounding islands, but he knew better.

He would have loved to slap a restraining order on his nearest neighbors under the threadbare cloak of ecological disturbance to wildlife, but even without binoculars he could see that nesting birds did not flee the roof of the caretaker's cottage behind the chapel, or even the offending bell tower during Chime Time.

MacKay alternately envied and despised such resiliency among less intelligent creatures than he. Human or otherwise.

As he tied up at Piscatawk Harbor, his mind wandered to the face of Elizabeth Will. No doubt about it. That was a condescending look she had cast like a baited hook in his direction. He wondered as objectively as he could if it might have been warranted. He wondered—subjectively—if Elizabeth Will might not be a woman entitled to look upon him in such a way. She had the assured carriage of a secret-bearer. He shed his idle musing with a shake of his shoulders, arching his chest to stretch out the tension in his back.

The tiny skiff had fought his navigational efforts for seven miles of open sea both ways. Fourteen miles of wrestling a steering wheel, and what for? Another verbal assault from Frank Will and a snotty attitude from his daughter?

"Dr. MacKay!"

What now? MacKay grumped to himself, climbing the viciously steep wooden stairway toward the research camp. Coping with the incline had built large, knotty muscles in his thighs that balanced the ropy bulk of the muscles through his chest, shoulders, and arms. A year of dredging, hauling, and diving had been beneficial to the athletic scientist; he had been lashed too long to a classroom. His appearance was not usually wasted on the equally fit young woman calling to him from the razor-wire fencing at the top of the stairs. Today she could not have cared less.

"What is it, Debra?" MacKay called up the gray crags. Gull droppings ran in rivulets toward the ocean and coated the banister with a thick crust.

"Last night," Debra Rothschilde shouted back, goose bumps rising on her bare thighs. She was upset, but not so upset that she would forget to flash her perfect legs at Charles MacKay. She almost always wore shorts, despite the cold winds. "It happened again last night."

"What happened?"

"He was back. The night visitor was at my window during the night." She hugged herself against the cold, shoulder-length fair hair blowing about her face.

MacKay sighed. Ghost sightings were so common among the inhabitants of the isles that witnesses rarely mentioned incidents. Debra did not accept the island superstitions very well, however. She was one of the youngest of the twenty or so research staff on Piscatawk, but one of the more clinical. Serious, he thought.

"The police are coming by this afternoon, Debra." MacKay reached the top of the climb, still breathing regularly. "Maybe they can put your mind at ease, once and for all." He was sick of discussing phantom Peeping Toms; he had work to do.

The island was as secure as twentieth-century technology and Mother Nature could make it. Razor wire necklaced the steep rocky ledges that plunged beneath the chop to the ocean floor. Sensors were set up at regular intervals around the perimeter to detect the sound or motion of advancing boats—either motor- or wind-driven. Unless an intruder swam in through seven miles of water that never broke forty-five degrees, there was no way to breach Piscatawk's security. The sensors were turned off during the day, but always engaged at night when Debra's imagined stalker appeared. Still, MacKay made an effort to be kind: the view of weathered headstones and the charred remains of fallen buildings from the window of a room in which one dreamed would give almost anyone the creeps. Except him, of course.

But understanding what made others tick was not his area of expertise. Let Chief Philbrick deal out the pop psychology. MacKay had hard science to keep him warm.

"Thank God," Debra breathed. MacKay noticed the graduate student's reddened eyes, tears re-forming and dropping from clotted lashes. Perhaps the isolation was getting to her. Maybe MacKay should have Ginny Philbrick take Debra back to the mainland with her. He could use a tougher assistant, anyway, though he would never find one smarter or prettier.

MacKay was not entirely heartless. It would not cost him much time to sympathize on the walk toward the dining hall. He had the taste of Frank Will's leekless stew to wash from his mouth.

"The police will check everything out, Debra. If there's anything to find, they'll find it."

"Oh, they'll find it, all right. I left it right where I found it this morning."

"Found what?"

Debra's voice quavered in syncopation with her trembling hands. "The body."

The young woman's voice was so measured and steady, it took a moment for MacKay to react. After grasping both of Debra's arms for a good look into her brown eyes, he released her and took off briskly in the direction of the dormitories. Over the sounds of wind and water, he heard her call to him.

"No, Dr. MacKay. Dr. MacKay, there's no dead *body.*" She trotted toward him as he slowed slightly. When she reached his side, she took his arm and panted, "Well, there *is* a body, but not a person." She drew a huge breath and finished. "It's a dead seagull. I moved it out of sight behind a grave marker."

MacKay wrestled down a sarcastic comment. If there were two things of which the islands had plenty, they were dead gulls and burial plots. His quandary regarding what was best for him and his high-strung assistant resolved itself easily. After she inspected the installation, he would ask Chief Philbrick to take his assistant back to shore to finish her studies at the main campus in Durham.

MacKay put a reassuring arm around the young woman's shoulder and gave himself a firm talking-to as they walked. Control was everything. Control was what he was best at.

"I'll take care of the gull myself," he offered.

"You don't understand, Doctor. I've seen dead seabirds hundreds of times. My undergraduate degree is in marine biology. That gull wasn't just lying around dead outside my bedroom window. It was nailed to sticks of driftwood and balanced on the sill during the night." Debra stopped walking and looked up into MacKay's eyes for emphasis. "The gull wasn't dead when it was put at my window. It was nailed down while it was still alive." She paused, looking away from MacKay and up into the sun. "It didn't stop screaming until nearly dawn."

"I'm sorry, Gin," Jesse apologized for the hundredth time since they had left his mooring. The police skiff dragged through the water behind the more stable forty-five-foot lobster boat. Unlike Frank Will's dilapidated commercial vessel, Jesse's was newly painted and perpetually scrubbed. Ginny wished her living room looked as clean as the floor slats on which she was balanced. The heavy boat broke the lulling swells with a hollow *chunk-chunk.* An irregular, lighter knocking came annoyingly from the cabin canopy above their heads. Ginny was bored with Jesse's remorse and did not bother to respond with yet another "forget it."

The bow of the *Celia T.* headed directly into the still-rising sun to the east and in the direction of the home of the boat's namesake, three miles beyond their destination. Who would ever have thought Jesse Kneeland would name his vessel for Celia Thaxter, Bard of Appledore Island? Both Jesse and Ginny had to put their jackets back on for the colder open sea air; leaving the harbor was like exiting a warm house into a wintery outdoors.

"See that?" Jesse asked, pointing to a small pile of boulders poking above the water. "That's where the offshore drilling guys found those gold doubloons. Most of the time, 'less the tide and moon are just right, you can't even see Drake's Rock, but there them coins were. Never found any others, though. Been there since the late fifteen hundreds, they figured. Pirates, you know."

Ginny nodded. She knew, just like every other native of the area. One of the great summer recreations had always been to take the kids out to the isles and grub around with metal detectors. Once Ginny had located a gold ring with a small ruby. Not pirate treasure; the ring had been dropped by some wealthy tourist sometime during the late nineteenth century. It was a pretty piece, though. She had given it to Sandy when the two of them had moved in together. It suited the smaller woman better and it was the most personal and romantic thing Ginny owned.

"Course, 'bout everybody had possession of the isles and the bank farther out at one time or other," Jesse continued passionately. Island history was practically the only thing Jesse seemed to care about—except, of course, Elizabeth Will. And it was obvious, even to him, that he got more encouragement from the islands. "Been inhabited since the time of Captain John Smith. Fishermen, mostly, but there have been plenty of families, too. Most of the old families hereabouts have done some time on the islands. My great-

great grandpa, for example, lived and died out there on Piscatawk. There were Philbricks there at that time, you know."

Ginny perked up a bit from her reverie. "Yeah?"

"Ayuh. Couple of Philbrick families. Before that, the Wills were scattered all the hell over, and the Jennesses, too. All the old families."

Bet Al Jenness would wish his kin had stayed out here, Ginny mused. Only two of the small isles were still privately owned, and only one of those had buildings still standing. The volunteer fire department had one by-jeezus trip out here to put out the flames every time a cottage or resort went up. Mostly Dovekey Beach's Bravest just stood on the town beach and watched the fire wave to them across the water.

Ginny knew that the two remaining settlements, the Eternal Sea Group on Piscatawk and the other, more intriguing community on Cap's Island, each had its own firefighting equipment. It was a condition of the states of New Hampshire and Maine, which governed in patchwork fashion as the boundaries fluctuated with the whims of historical research.

Lucky Ginny. The newest boundaries put the docking area at Piscatawk in her jurisdiction. Two years ago, it would have been the problem of the Kittery Maniacs.

"When was the last time you got onto Cap's Island, Jesse?" Ginny asked.

"Well, hell's bells. Ain't nobody local been on that island since, hell, nineteen-sixty-something. My daddy spent lots of time out there, though. Said it were the prettiest of the bunch." Jesse looked embarrassed at his lack of specifics.

"Nobody local at all?" Ginny questioned.

"Nope," he answered. "Nobody I ever heard. Even the maids and such is brought in from out of state."

Jesse would have known, too, if anyone from town had visited. She thought she knew why the Dovekey Beachers stayed away in droves, but it would not hurt to be sure. So insular were the Cap's Island inhabitants that she had not fully considered what they might have seen or noticed the night of Al Jenness's untimely demise. *Sloppy police work,* she chided herself. *Getting too damned comfortable.* She owed a lot to Al Jenness. He had done much in the last few months to reintroduce her best friend, Biz, to the community in her own right, instead of as "one of those Will girls."

The way he had died was not nice. His burial at sea was not comfortable.

Besides, it was ludicrous for a police chief to have responsibility for a territory she had never even seen, populated by a group of seasonal citizens nobody knew.

But if the inhabitants of Cap's Island had waited thirty or so years for a courtesy call, they could wait until Ginny Philbrick was through with Dr. MacKay.

Piscatawk Island glared dully at the *Celia T.* as Ginny roped a mooring post to pull the boat in. After lashing the police skiff, she waved Jesse off and watched him head around east of Piscatawk and north. Since he was not tramping around the larger Isle of Shoals three miles farther out to sea, he must be taking the scenic route back around west to Smith's Isle, past Cap's.

Ginny's navigational skills extended only far enough to get her to and from her territories. The crippling banks beyond these islets were a mystery to her, but she supposed Jesse knew what he was doing. He did not know much, but he was a seaman.

Ginny felt the presence of Cap's Island over her left shoulder and shuddered in the sudden breeze.

NINE

ELIZABETH AND AVIS sat in the kitchen watching their father putter. He was whistling show tunes from the 1940s.

"Okay, offspring, make yourselves useful and get out the good soup bowls. We don't have enough of the pottery ones." Frank had a peculiar fastidiousness about matching place settings.

"Yes, we do," Elizabeth said. "Unless Petunia is joining us at the table." The dog opened one eye in response to her name, then went back to sleep.

"It's time you knew, Lizzie. Petunia's a *dog.*"

"Could have fooled me," Avis chimed in.

"Get out the good dishes," Frank repeated.

"We have three of the pottery bowls, Dad."

"I know that. We need six. We don't have six of the pottery bowls. So get out the china."

Avis got up and went to the china cabinet across the room. "I told you, Dad, the kids are out of town with their father."

Frank turned away from the steaming pot on the stove and faced his children. He counted on his fingers: "Me, one; Lizzie, two; Avis, three; Jesse, four; Ginny, five; Sandy, six. Any more questions?"

"Dad," Elizabeth protested, "you heard Ginny. She can't be hanging around with us until the investigation is over. Weren't you listening to anything?"

"She'll be here," Frank assured her. "Just get out the china, Number Two Daughter. Number One Daughter, try to find the poker chips. I feel lucky."

MacKay stared at the broken body of the gull splayed across the crossed sticks. Aluminum roofing nails protruded from the wings and webbed feet. The bird's extremities were splattered red on white, red on gray, where the blood had sprayed during its frantic death throes. There was no doubt that the impalement had occurred while the animal was still living. The white head lolled limply to one side, eyes open to the scrub grass on which the sad thing lay.

"My God," MacKay whispered.

"I told you," muttered Debra. "I told you, and you didn't listen. I knew it wasn't my imagination."

"I guess not." But he still was not convinced. He would reserve judgment until after Ginny had seen the island and put in her two cents' worth. It was, after all, just a gull, and he had a lot of work to accomplish before the summer semester began.

"Dr. MacKay?"

He swung around to face the sharp crease of Ginny Philbrick's slacks.

"May I take a look?" Ginny lowered herself beside him. MacKay nodded as she knelt on the sea grass and leaned over the mutilated body of the gull. Debra watched, shivering, her arms crossed protectively in front of her body. "Well, well," Ginny murmured, poking the gull with a pen from her shirt pocket.

"What do you think, Chief?" MacKay asked.

"I think," answered Ginny, pulling herself upright, "that people were *very* busy last night."

★ ★ ★

Jesse held the copy of the old nautical map away from the sun and compared it to a small leather-bound book. A metal detector hung from a twine sling over his back. Several times he checked the map against the book and squinted from north to south. With a dull shrug, the lobsterman plodded northeast over the scrub and sedge grass, the metal detector bouncing and banging against his left calf with each step.

Today, he promised himself, he would locate the old gravesite and find what he needed. The garden trowel he had picked up at the flea market the Saturday before slipped out of his sweatshirt pocket and bounced off his heavy rubber-soled boots. Picking it up, he spotted a likely area slightly beyond where he had planned to dig. He reprimanded himself for a foolish purchase. The hands of a commercial lobsterman were tougher than most forged metal.

Still, he owed some fripperies to himself.

And he had a sickening feeling he owed much more than that to Frank Will, or would soon.

TEN

After laying out the dining room table (for six) with the good china, Elizabeth and Avis left their father entertaining himself at the stove and went out to check on the overly ambitious garden space behind the house.

The snap peas were well up, pods set. Lettuce, spinach, and kale made hazy green suggestions in the wet soil. Elizabeth earnestly set to turning over the earth with a sharpened spade at the farthest corner from the house. Avis studied the seedlings hardening off in the cold frame.

"No zucchini, Biz." Avis waited for an explosive response. She wanted the comfort of her sister's overreaction. She wanted her old family back.

"I hate squash," Elizabeth replied calmly. Avis's heart rose happily. "Besides, zucchini is for amateurs," Elizabeth continued. "If every moron on the East Coast couldn't grow it, there would be no zucchini bread, zucchini pickles, or damned zucchini festivals."

Avis's hopes were dashed. If she could not provoke her eminently provokable sister on the subject of the number one most despised vegetable on the Will family hit list, there was no hope. None that day, in any event. She looked toward the kitchen window. Frank was standing at the sink, his lips puckered in song. Hopeless. Frank: manic. Elizabeth: implacable. Avis glanced up once again and then wandered casually to her sister's side.

"He's awfully happy, isn't he?"

"Sure is," Elizabeth responded noncommittally. She handed the spade to Avis and picked up a hoe to break up clods of heavy spring dirt. "Unnaturally so, wouldn't you say?"

"I would." Avis rammed the spade into the ground, waiting for an elaboration that did not come. "You know, I really hate to ask—I mean *really* hate to ask—but was Dad home last night?"

Elizabeth pulled herself to her full height and looked into Avis's eyes. "He was back here from the Town Meeting before I was."

Avis shook her head wearily. "Yes," she persisted, "but did he *stay* home?"

The two women studied one another carefully, seeming to reach a mutual decision.

"I have no idea," Elizabeth answered, and whacked the moist ground hard enough that Avis could feel the impact reverberate through the soles of her rubber shoes.

"Boy. I was afraid of that."

"Well, you know what it's like around here since Mom jumped ship. I've gotten so used to Dad rattling around at all hours and taking his midnight jaunts to God knows where, I don't even hear the door when he goes out anymore. If I did, I'd never get any sleep at all." Part of Elizabeth's strategy for behaving more rationally than anyone else in her family was to get at least eight hours' sleep per night. Until now, it had nearly worked.

"I know," Avis said soothingly. "It's just that, well, Dad has been peculiar ever since Mom left—"

"More peculiar," Elizabeth interjected.

"More peculiar," Avis agreed. "Do you think he's finally

gone round the bend? This perky, peppy, zippy act is giving me the spooks. It's not natural, under the circumstances."

"The circumstances weren't exactly natural, either."

"So?"

"So, I guess we wait to see who's coming to dinner."

Frank Will appeared in the back doorway, slipping on a ratty red plaid flannel jacket, cocker spaniel at his heels. His daughters looked toward him guiltily and quickly resumed battering the top-soil.

"I left the stew on simmer. Think you can keep it from boiling over or should I turn it off?" he asked.

Avis reacted a little too instantly for Elizabeth's taste. No wonder the younger sister always got caught when she was up to something. "Where are you going?"

"Thought I'd clear the winter off Lyddie back there." He nodded toward the back woods. There was a small family plot tucked into the juncture of two stone walls that had been haphazardly tended since the last funeral, in 1882. That was for Lydia Will, Frank's great-great grandmother.

"I can do that, Dad," Avis offered.

"My job," Frank said. "Be yours soon enough."

"Want company?" Avis persisted. Frank scowled in discouragement.

"Have Lyddie to talk to. You can find me later if you're so intent on bonding. Gonna work on the traps and could use some help. Seems like I'm gonna be one shy for a while now." His daughters tried not to cringe at Frank's offhand comment about the confiscated and unavailable pot. "Damned bureaucrats. C'mon, Petunia." He slapped his thigh to get the attention of the cocker spaniel, who was trying to find something good to eat about a stranded, bloated earthworm. On the second call, the dog gave up.

Elizabeth and Avis watched their father and Petunia, a stray floral gardening glove now flopping from her mouth, amble into the pine forest.

Until then, both women had believed that nothing their father could do would shock them. But Frank Will doing nothing to instigate tumult from his neighbors or close relatives was terribly shocking. It was the only real hobby they had known him to enjoy.

Life is full of surprises, thought Avis. *And so is death.*

Elizabeth leaned on her grimy spade. The last of the forsythia blossoms were hurling themselves from the whips to which they clung in the wake of Frank and Petunia's exit.

He can't bait me, Elizabeth vowed. *Not this time.*

Ginny blew the electronic horn on the police skiff three times as she pulled away from Piscatawk Island's dock.

She knew that the picture of the tormented gull would stay with her for a long time—popping up in dreams and during wool-gathering. Ginny had seen very few gull corpses: the seabirds are cannibalistic, and earthly remains are quickly served up as dinner. Not knowing exactly why, she wrapped the bird's carcass in a plastic bag from the ESG kitchen for examination later. *Cheery prospect.*

Unbidden, the memory of Al Jenness's hands, stripped to the bone, flashed through her mind, and she fingered the copy of his note in her pocket.

The ocean: recycling in action.

Now, *that* would be some slogan for the Dovekey Beach Chamber of Commerce.

Ginny kept the throttle at about five knots, staying close to the south shore of the islets. Her next stop was no more than half a mile west of Charles MacKay's encampment, and she wanted time to formulate a few questions.

The dormitory buildings on Piscatawk all faced north, away from the area where Al Jenness had been pulled up, so none of the Eternal Sea Group techies had seen anything out of the ordinary the night before—except, of course, poor Debra. The gull incident was obviously the result of a personnel problem on Piscatawk. Unless neighboring islanders could walk on water, there was no other way a person could get to the Eternal Sea Group laboratories to harass the girl. Clearly, an in-house job.

The folks next door on Cap's were Ginny's last chance to locate an eyewitness. For Frank Will's sake, she hoped there was an insomniac among the visitors or staff.

Charles MacKay locked himself in his office with strict orders that he not be disturbed. He was testy, and knew enough to keep away from the delicate sensibilities of his fellow academics. He worked an intricate game of cat's cradle, winding the fingers of both hands into a loop of twine, manipulating design after design.

The gull was a melodramatic touch, he thought. A bit over the edge, perhaps, but clever. He could never understand why civilians thought scientists had no imagination.

The security system checked out, as he had known it would. He had overseen it himself, going so far as to insist that the razor wire be hung just below water level where the island dipped. No one would believe that an intruder could be stupid enough to dive from a boat out of range of the sensors and swim in.

A sour snort escaped MacKay as he rubbed his eyes with the backs of his wrists. If it had been his nature, he would have laughed at himself. For all the planning, for all the hours of work, it had never occurred to him that there might be a threat from within. *Stress, isolation, like being wrapped in a wet sheet. Stupid not to realize.*

MacKay looped his fingers in and around the cat's cradle and pulled his hands apart. The tenuous structure fell to hammocky ribbons from his long, callused fingers.

Stupid. Anyone can snap.

★   ★   ★

Bells. Ginny checked her watch. Mickey Mouse said it was three-thirty. Her stomach rumbled. The few trees that grew on Cap's Island cut the afternoon wind enough that Ginny unzipped her jacket for the walk toward Victorian Hotel, glowering from the highest point of land ahead. Three stories of blindingly white clapboard, celery-green ornamental woodwork, and knife-sharp forest-green shutters thrust from the pile of rock like a white-gloved hand from beneath a landslide. Remains of an earlier, shorter-lived hotel lay north and west of the stone caretaker's cottage reflected in the sparkling six-over-six windows. Jesse's rather poetic characterization, "it were the prettiest of the bunch," came to mind. The difference between the new and improved Piscatawk and the left-alone Cap's Island was remarkable.

She could see three middle-aged women and one man sitting in the rattan rockers that dotted the circular porch. They were reading, chatting, doing the things tourists do on secluded islands. Except rocking. The four residents sat stock-still. When Ginny was within a hundred feet of the entrance, one of the women got up and disappeared into the lobby, the screen door making a *slap, slap, slap* behind her. Even then, her vacated chair did not move. Ginny wondered whether the rockers had been nailed to the porch decking and then rejected the idea as paranoia—and not laughable at that. No one in the world believed rocking was a sin.

The bells stopped their taunting clamor, spreading a flannel sheet of vast quiet rumpled only by the scrunching of Ginny's rubber-soled deck shoes on the crushed-seashell path. She glanced down as her ankles wobbled over the uneven surface.

Long-evacuated periwinkles, slipper shells, razor clams, fractured bits of sea urchin: a decorative walk built on dead things. That was the way of the islands.

At the base of the porch stairs, Ginny paused. The guests continued to sit unconcerned, immobile, reading or staring out at the horizon as though the Dovekey Beach chief of police had mastered the trick of invisibility.

"Excuse me," Ginny prompted, getting no reaction whatsoever. *"Excuse* me." The nonrockers turned their heads slowly in her direction. No curiosity registered at the appearance of a female police officer standing eight feet away, seven miles out to sea.

"Well, well," said the man as he opened the screen door of the hotel and stepped out onto the enameled porch deck. "Well, well," he repeated, and held out his hand for Ginny to shake. He was late-middle-aged, medium height, with medium brown hair thinning at the back of his pate, moderately overweight, wearing khakis that drooped just a bit low under the stomach, a white cotton shirt and green bow tie. A man so average he was distinctive, with a smile that reached no higher than his nostrils. Ginny walked up the stairs and shook his outstretched hand.

"Chief Lavinia Philbrick," she introduced herself, a bit taken aback that the man's hand was dry and warm. She had prepared herself for a damp, flaccid touch. "And you are?"

"The Reverend Garrett Selby, shepherd to this island flock." He gave a flourish of an arm movement that enclosed everything in sight. "How nice of you to make a call. I don't think we've had a mainland visitor here since, well . . ."

"Never?"

"Oh, well, I don't think *that* long. Perhaps, though. Perhaps." He chuckled. "Well, well."

The hairs on the back of Ginny's neck stood up. Something about Selby made her distinctly uncomfortable—queasy, even. It was a visceral discomfort based on no hard information whatsoever. Having been judged in that fashion herself, Ginny made the effort to clear her mind and start over.

"Yes," she said, "it has certainly been long enough, hasn't it?"

Reverend Selby remained planted like a potted palm in his spot outside the door. "Yes, yes, it has. Well, as they say, better late than never, eh?" The congregation members continued their reading and staring out to sea, pages unturned and pupils fixed. Ginny checked her watch.

"If you have a few minutes, Reverend Selby, I'd like to talk with you. There was an incident near here this morning, and I need to know if you or any of your guests saw anything."

"Incident?" Selby parroted, still not moving.

"Murder, Reverend Selby," Ginny corrected herself, impatient once again in her distaste for the religious leader. Antsy in the presence of so much immobility. Agitated around prescribed calm. The rocking-chair contingent remained impassive. "Is there somewhere we can talk?"

"Well. Well, of course," Selby said. He pulled the screen door open and indicated with a nod that they should go inside. "Of course."

He led Ginny through a lobby area larger than she had anticipated, featuring, if not furniture, some of the finest parquet flooring she had seen in the area. It gleamed the way old hardwoods will when well loved and tended. Probably teak, she judged, to have escaped the almost inevitable damage from air saturated with salt over the course of more than a hundred years.

Selby continued to the right, beyond a graceful sweep of banister and stair, down a short corridor, and opened a heavily carved oak door into a room in which two windows faced out on the ocean and the distant shore. A third window, at the rear, framed the caretaker's cottage as perfectly as a painting. The windows, so well proportioned from the exterior, proved to stand no less than six feet high. Light that might have been discouraged in another site bounced with joy off the walls of polished shelving. Books of every age, with bindings of all colors, glowed in the warmth of that room. Two crewel-embroidered wingback chairs, somewhat the worse for wear, flanked a forest-green moiré sofa from the late Victorian era. Horsehair stuffing, no doubt, which accounted for the superior condition of the upholstery. The sort of furniture only a Victorian could spend any time sitting on without hours of therapy from a qualified chiropractor. Beautiful, nonetheless.

To Ginny's right, against the wall that the damaging sun never reached, were hundreds of leather-bound volumes. A faint odor of mildew wafted from the collection. The rows lined up like old veterans, elbow to elbow; stragglers too tall or fat pushed their way into formation as best they could. Each, no doubt, had a lifetime of war stories to tell, should anyone be interested enough to ask.

Ginny crossed the threshold in front of the minister, who shut the door tightly behind them. She reached for a black leather portfolio, closed with black cord.

"May I?" She wanted a closer look.

"I'm sorry," Selby said, taking her arm. "These volumes are so old, we don't handle them unless absolutely necessary. It would be a crime to do any harm out of mere curiosity, don't you think?"

But still no one swayed to comfort themselves in the startlingly white rockers' arms.

Jesse knelt at the top of the small rise and pulled at the mat of moss he had loosened with the gardening tool he had brought along. It came up with the muffled tearing sound of old Velcro.

Jesse searched beneath the moss carpet for the presence of milled granite; earwigs scurried over his soiled hands as he dug deeper.

Swearing under his breath, apologizing to the wind for his loss of temper, Jesse sat back in frustration. There was granite beneath the shallow cover of soil, but it was merely the unquarried ledge that composed the base of the small island. A simple eight-foot obelisk cast a long shadow from the cemetery on an adjoining hill.

It was getting very late.

★　★　★

"So," Selby finished, standing to dismiss Ginny, "I will be happy to ask the congregation if anyone did see anything last evening, though I'm sure it would have been mentioned." Ginny stood, too, reluctant to leave the wonderful room but wanting a cigarette badly.

"They may not have known it was important."

"True, true," Selby clucked, leading the way to the door. "True, true."

The sun was descending rapidly, and Ginny turned for one last glimpse of the caretaker's cottage framed in the window.

"Do you keep the cottage so perfect just for the view from this window?" she asked.

"It is perfect, isn't it?" Selby answered. "But we keep Will's Cottage up for year-round use. It isn't practical to heat this monolith during the winter when so few guests visit."

"Will's Cottage?"

Selby continued to the door and opened it. "Old name. Everyone calls it that. Probably built by some William Something-or-other originally and it's all been forgotten."

Or someone named Something-or-other Will, she reasoned without joy at the thought.

"Thank you, Reverend Selby," she said as she left the library, thinking a thousand uninvited things.

"My pleasure," Selby answered, not pleased with his thought process either, and closed himself back inside the darkening room.

ELEVEN

SANDY WAS THE first to arrive and the last to know. She thought that typical and did not take it personally.

The back door was open, so she let herself into the kitchen and pulled a beer out of the 1950s refrigerator and set it by the sink while she washed her hands. There was a combination of plaster and unknown black material lodged under her short oval nails. Gritty Lava soap would remove just about anything, and she had known there would be some under the old porcelain sink, so rather than stop at the corner store to buy a cake, she had waited to wash.

The smell of lobster stew raised a symphony of rumblings in her stomach. Her hands were lathered all the way up to her elbows when she heard the door bang open. The cold gust of air raised goose bumps along her wet arms.

"Want to stir that stew, or did you just come by to shower?" Frank dumped a pile of twine in the corner by the door before lifting the top of the soup pot. He let out a delighted sigh at the aroma. "Damn, but I'm good."

"Hi, honey, I'm home," Sandy replied, rinsing off her soapy arms and reaching for her beer.

"Thanks," Frank said, lifting the bottle from her fingers. "Tough day at the office?"

Sandy shook back her curly, dirty-blond hair and got another beer out of the refrigerator. "Nope. Just the usual. How about you, Frank?"

"Same shit, different day," Frank replied and saluted her with his beer. "Except for Jenness, of course." He pronounced the last word "cause." Sandy perked up; Frank only put on a New England accent when he was attempting to be laid-back and casual. If Frank was intent on pursuing his Town Meeting altercation further, it would just put Ginny in a piss-poor mood for their poker game.

"What have you done, Frank?" Sandy asked, knowing how much he relished sharing stories of the annoying escapades he perpetrated on his unsuspecting neighbors.

"You haven't heard?" Frank looked genuinely surprised. Sandy could only assume that this meant he had done something *really* wicked. The sort of long drawn-out yarn-spinning for which he was notorious—the sort she recounted to her disbelieving family in Lancaster County, Pennsylvania. They were, of course, normal, unlike Frank.

"What? Heard what?"

Frank sipped his beer with infuriating slowness. He was enjoying himself. Sandy could see him stifling a smirk. She played his game and repeated herself.

"Frank. What did you do?"

He gave in to the grin. "I murdered the old crud," he answered, got up from the table, and stirred the stew himself.

Jesse's face was illuminated in lumps and pockets by the dials and running lights. It was the time of the evening when the moon has not yet fully risen, but the sunken sun gives only the dullest glow from behind the water's horizon. It made Jesse feel as if he were swimming through an oppressive green-gray murk of hazy light.

It was also the time of day when body temperatures drop and a chill will germinate inside a man's skin, seeming to grow from the bone outward.

Jesse hunched his shoulders against the wind and pushed the throttle full ahead. The knit cap he kept on board had gotten wet on the floor of the boat, and short of encasing his head in oily rags from the hold, the best he could do was get to shore before he started to shudder himself sick.

He had been so certain that today he would find the proof he was looking for on Cap's Island. Frank would be so pleased with him.

And, eventually, so would Elizabeth. He clutched the warm antique silver coin his metal detector had discovered at the site of the old cemetery. It was a pretty one, and it had not been buried too deep, either. That was a good sign, he figured. It would be so pretty hung on a silver chain around Elizabeth's neck.

He wanted to give her the coin right away. He really wanted to see the look on her face. He was not sure he could wait long enough for a jeweler to put it on a chain. That was all right, too. *Sometimes a man waits, and sometimes a man just cannot.*

Jesse hummed an old Beatles song to the *thunk-thunk-thunk* from the cabin roof that had so irritated Ginny but now sounded musically in tandem with the thud of the bow hitting each wave on the way to shore.

The bells chimed out the Evensong service and the Children of Deity answered the call. The Reverend Garrett Selby stood at the open door to the church greeting one and all despite the cold. He knew none of his people would be late. It was not allowed.

After the oldest and slowest parishioner had been welcomed and seated in the simple Congregationalist-style place of worship, Selby took his position at the head of the room, in front of the altar. Plain multipaned windows stood like an honor guard along the expanse of newly whitewashed walls, front to back. Behind the altar, only a sanguine damask fabric stretched floor to ceiling—straight and stiff as Garrett Selby himself. There was no microphone; Selby had never needed one. Despite his less than athletic appearance, the reverend had the voice of an NFL quarterback.

The congregation that faced him was a disparate group. There were the usual elderly in search of solace on the last sprint of their race toward eternity, but there were also a good number of the pious in their early twenties, and a less representational smattering of those in between who like to plan ahead.

If Ginny Philbrick thought her sudden presence on Cap's Island had caused no curiosity or concern, she was dead wrong.

The island of seriously homogeneous minds had awakened that morning to unnerving boat traffic just as it turned light. Shouts across expanses of water travel with eerie clarity for unnerving distances. On the mainland, the commotion would have sent nearly all the residents to their television sets for a news update and a little vicarious living, but worldly items such as radios and televisions were forbidden on Cap's Island. Prayer and introspection were required for admission to the Children of Deity's retreat. Matters other than the spiritual were relegated to discussion strictly in the presence of the church elders—if then—and the rotating populations of the island were disciplined ones, not given to rule-breaking.

But a pledge of silence did not stop them from thinking, no matter how much (each in his or her own way) it might have slowed them down.

The seventy-five worshippers and staff of eight shifted in the cushionless pews and waited as patiently as they could for properly delivered illumination. The old stone chapel had no heat or insulation, which suited Selby fine. It kept the sanctioned discussions short and sweet.

"Brothers and Sisters," he began, keeping his voice low and

slow, "today I received some very sad news." The congregation looked earnest and leaned subtly forward in their seats. "Though we all commit ourselves to taking our time upon this island to refocus on the spiritual, eschewing secular life, rejecting the corruption and filth of the out-people, it is my sad duty to have to acquaint you all with an unavoidable reminder of the putrescence which surrounds us in our innocence. I do this not out of joy, nor as an object lesson, but because—until the time of the cleansing—we all are forced to rise above the sludge of the satanic majority."

Selby paused for another requisite round of "Amens." Mix up the routine with the uncommon, he always said. Acceptance of one early precept can lead, logically and step by step, to the acceptance of the truth that the moon is made of green cheese. He focused his voice to bounce from the farthest corners of the whitewashed walls.

"There has been a murder—an *untimely* death in the waters just off our island." By just the slightest fraction, Selby increased the tone and tempo of his speech.

"I say untimely," he continued, "though nothing is untimely in *God's wisdom*." He waited for another "Amen" from his audience, then plunged ahead, riding the fervent tide downward and then up. "The bureaucratic powers that be are convinced that there is punishment here on earth. They *believe*"—he paused once again, just for a second—"they *believe* that the evil man does may be atoned for in this lifetime." His face reflected the idiocy of such thinking. He searched the faces of his listeners for mirror images of shock and disdain. As heads began to shake in disbelief, his voice pierced the buzz, louder and stronger. "We know better.

"We know better, because we *are* better! We have given ourselves up to the *will of God!*"

Murmurs of agreement built as the reverend waited. They swelled to a roll of ecstatic moans, and then to shouts of fervid confirmation. At their height, Garrett Selby projected his voice over and down through the cacophony; the voice burned its way through the din like a shaft of lightning through a rainstorm.

"But we have seen *nothing*. We know nothing of the pus that infects the wounds of the festering masses because *we* are *clean*. Our eyes do not *acknowledge* the excrement in which the out-people *wallow*. It is *not* ours to *see*."

The oldest parishioner, a fragile, papery woman in her nineties, began to rock, her knotted hands covering her eyes. Those around her picked up the rhythm. Quickly Selby took full possession of his stage, leaning toward his rapt listeners.

"Is this our way?" he shouted.

"No!" came the smattering of responses.

"Do we see the *filth* of the *damned?*"

"No!"

Amid the Children of Deity's chanting, Garrett Selby wiped his face of the perspiration that coursed from his pasty brow to his white collar. He nodded in time with his parishioners' *"No, no, no"* and looked over their heads into the watering eyes of Eli, his baby brother, standing in the doorway. The contented smile of a job well done stretched Garrett Selby's thin lips to a hard zipper.

Eli sighed, wishing to the high heavens he were back in Boston. That, unfortunately, was not possible for a while. And as much as he despised Cap's Island and everything about it, it was better than his limited alternatives.

No. He wouldn't tell.

No way in hell.

TWELVE

AFTER NEARLY KILLING herself tripping over the tangle of twine
Frank had left by the door, Ginny was the last to scoop a ladleful of
lobster stew into the good china she got from the dining room table
and sit herself down at the Formica kitchen table. Only Elizabeth
glanced up with any surprise at Ginny's arrival.

The game was well under way, poker chips long used up and
oyster crackers pressed into duty as legal currency. The only "serious" money anywhere in sight was an eighteenth-century silver
coin incongruously placed next to Elizabeth's beer bottle.

"Seven-card Mexican Sweat," Jesse proclaimed as he dealt the
cards.

"Jeez," Elizabeth protested.

"That's 'no-seezies,'" Frank corrected Jesse.

"It's a girl's game," Elizabeth muttered. "No skill. Jeez." She
threw in her ante: one oyster cracker. All the plastic chips were in
front of Frank, the card-counter from hell.

"Jeez," echoed Avis, tossing in her cracker.

"I like no-seezies." Sandy supported Jesse and accepted a kiss
on the cheek from Ginny. She, too, was reduced to wagering with

baked goods but was so accustomed to losing her shirt that it did not bother her in the slightest.

"Deal you in, Ginny?" Frank asked.

"Nahhh," Ginny answered, and pulled up a stool to the table. "It's a girl's game." She unbuckled her shoulder holster and placed it and her service revolver on the shelf above the sink, and kicked the offending twine trap into a corner before sitting. She took a tentative taste of the lobster stew and watched the game unfold, Sandy going first. Might as well; she didn't have a prayer of winning a hand, since she characteristically insisted on playing for fun.

"Was on Cap's Island this afternoon," Ginny said while Sandy tried to get into some charmed communication with her cards.

"Cap's?" Jesse's head shot up.

"Ayuh," Ginny affirmed. "Your pop was right, Jess, it were the prettiest of the bunch. Think so, Frank?"

"Haven't been on her since 'thirty-nine, but 'spect you're right."

Sandy finished her lucky ritual and threw down her first card. And lost.

"Hah!" Frank said.

Avis was the second to try. She had to beat the upturned ten covering the original jack. The odds were lousy. She shrugged amiably and got up to pour another glass of white wine before subjecting herself to ignominious defeat. Ginny filled the time.

"Not since 'thirty-nine, Frank? I figured since it's called Will's Cottage, that little stone house behind the main building belonged to your family." Elizabeth leaned forward on the table but said nothing. Avis was struggling to find room in the refrigerator to put away the gallon jug of Gallo *vin très ordinaire.*

"Was," Frank acceded easily. "Hasn't been a Will living there since 'eighty-two, though." Elizabeth leaned in even farther. "Eighteen eighty-two, that is, when Great-great-gramma Lyddie moved here to the mainland. She's buried out back, if you want to check to make sure she's dead."

"Believe you, Frank," Ginny said. Elizabeth leaned back in her chair. Avis returned to her place with a fresh glass of wine and lost her turn in two tries.

Elizabeth turned her first card dubiously and won that match off.

"No wonder you're so against any building out there, Frank. Family homestead and all," Ginny persisted.

"Not my business," Frank answered. "Just don't want a sin industry in my backyard." Sensing an unhappy conclusion to a pleasant evening, Jesse butted in to smooth the choppy water.

"All them royal grants and such were called off during the War of 1812, Gin. Whatchucallit, nullified. You can check at the Athenaeum for the actual records. All us have had a shitload of time to get used to strangers on the islands."

"No, thanks, Jess. I'll take your word for it."

"May I play my cards, *please?*" Elizabeth snapped. Her second and third cards also won. Ginny watched her friend's apathy turn to cold competitiveness, even though seven-card Mexican Sweat had nothing whatsoever to do with skill. It was the definitive game of chance. Elizabeth's fourth card was a loser, and she spat a colorful epithet. She also grabbed Jesse's pouch of tobacco and expertly rolled herself a cigarette. By the time he fumbled a matchbook out to do the gentlemanly thing, Elizabeth was already puffing away furiously.

Stressed out, Ginny commented to herself. *The slippery slope of nicotine addiction and living with Frank Will.*

"Don't matter to Frank," Jesse started in once more.

"Are we playing cards or what?" Elizabeth said.

Frank stretched his arms and reached for the card on the top of his pile. He feinted, and stretched again. It was an old Art Carney

Honeymooners bit. Jesse laughed nervously, as he always did at Frank's wit.

"Father!" Elizabeth snapped in frustration. Ginny finished her stew and went back to the stove for seconds.

"Pretty good, eh, Chief?" Frank asked, knowing it was.

"Dad, are you playing or what?" Avis asked irritably.

Ginny noted the sisters' annoyance. It was not the companionable razzing she was used to over Wednesday-night gambling.

Frank either didn't notice, or chose not to. He played out the remainder of his cards in rapid fire, apparently never doubting the Will luck.

"Ah-ha!" he said. "Old age and guile win out one more time." With that he swept the mishmash of pennies, nickels, and oyster crackers into a pile in front of him. Collecting the cards, he started an expert shuffle, shooting his best, most malevolent cardshark look at everyone around the table. "You in, Philbrick?" Ginny nodded and he dealt, calling the game. "Five-card stud. Dime ante."

Jesse groaned, pulled out a dollar bill, and made change out of Frank's winnings. Sandy held out her hand for the coins in Ginny's pocket but got only half.

Ginny wondered whether anyone was going to ask.

"So, Ginny." Frank threw down the gauntlet along with the six hands of Hoyle cards. "Your honorable presence here this evening can only mean one thing." He looked at his cards and threw in another dime. Ignoring the fact that none of the other players had tossed in, he continued, "I'll take one."

"What would that be, Frank?" Ginny asked, throwing in her dime. "I'll take two."

Frank dealt Ginny's two. "That I no longer languish under the cloud of suspicion." *Leave it to Frank to stick his head directly into the lion's mouth,* thought Ginny.

Elizabeth was livid. The color in her cheeks rose so high, it

84

seemed to levitate the dusting of freckles an inch from her face. She tossed the cards, at which she had not even looked, into the center of the table and went to the liquor cabinet to pour herself a shot of Maker's Mark bourbon. She swallowed with a neat snapping back of her head and poured herself another. Everyone pretended not to notice. Especially Avis, who knew better.

This was the moment Frank had been waiting for. If Elizabeth took the bait, another of those verbal free-for-alls her father cherished above all other human interactions would result. Her stomach would end up in the kind of knot Houdini wouldn't have been able to unsnarl and Frank would blow off every bit of tension he had ever owned and spend the night sleeping like a baby. Well, Elizabeth was not going to play this time. Not poker, and not capital punishment roulette.

Avis tried valiantly to keep her voice low enough that Elizabeth would not hear. "Is that right, Gin?"

Elizabeth grimaced, tossed back the second shot of bourbon, grabbed the bottle by its innocent neck, and let it dangle by her side. She pleaded silently with her sister to keep her mouth shut. Everyone knew that if you left a dog alone with a chocolate cake on the floor the dog would eat the cake. So you do not leave chocolate cakes on a dog's floor and you do not, for God's sake, ask the dog where the cake is if you do leave it there and it is gone when you get back. *Shut up, Avis. Wait and see if the dog gets the shits. Then you know, without having made an ass of yourself.*

Ginny seemed to be on the psychic plane and did not answer Avis's or Frank's question as she pondered her poker hand, correctly figuring she was in a two-handed game.

"Is that right, Gin?" Jesse asked eagerly. "Did you find something out this afternoon? Do you have a suspect?"

Avis examined her hand just as though she were playing it, which she was not. Elizabeth stood behind Jesse and squeezed the heavy deltoid muscle over his shoulder until another man would have screeched in abject pain. Jesse simply covered her hand with his and smiled up at her gratefully.

"Your bet, Frank," Ginny said and rearranged the cards in her right hand one more time.

"Quarter." Frank threw in.

Ginny bet her quarter, looked directly at Frank, and said, "See you."

Frank turned over his hand. A pair of queens stared up at the graying ceiling fixture that had come with the kitchen update in 1949. The light reflected off the dusty framed marine charts that had hung in the same spot for years longer than that.

Ginny flipped her five cards, one at a time. Two pair, jacks high.

"You lose, Frank," Ginny said.

The fireproof lockbox lay open on the coffee table next to a lead-crystal decanter of good Porto. A guttering bayberry candle cast a languid glow over the varied surfaces: cut glass, burnished cherry-wood, and die-cast metal.

Ruth Jenness reclined as though professionally posed on the luxuriantly upholstered camelback sofa in the formal living room. A small fire danced a hornpipe beneath the mahogany mantel, making the tidy pile of folded papers beside the sofa seem to keep time to the classical background music. Ruth sipped at her lead-crystal aperitif glass of ruby wine, careful not to spill on her special alone-time ivory satin peignoir.

The insurance papers were in order. Between the two policies Al had taken out—and the one she had authorized without his knowledge on the better than even chance that he had not provided adequately for her in the event of his unfortunate demise—Ruth would be coming into about two hundred thousand dollars. The mortgage on the house—she excused herself—*both* mortgages on the house would be covered as well. *That* was a relief, at least.

Ruth poured another full measure of port to steady herself. The heavy liquor would make a dent in the hole she felt in her life.

The hole was not caused by the absence of Al Jenness, now in transit from the morgue slab in Concord to the Buckmaster Funeral Home in Portsmouth.

It was caused by the papers she knew had *not* lain in the fire-proof lockbox now spayed open like a gutted cod on her polished Queen Anne coffee table.

THIRTEEN

THE BREAKFAST 'N' BEANS parking lot was filled, though it was past nine A.M. and well beyond the morning rush. Though the name of the coffee shop advertised something more than the first meal of the day, aside from a second, moderately busy sandwich crowd at noon, eggs were the big draw at the B 'n' B. Served up with a healthy side of town gossip. Refills on the house.

The building looked like a refurbished gas station, which it was, one of the fancy big ones with a peaked slate roof and weathervane. Vinnie Bartlett, the owner, had added an additional seating section off at the side and named it the Moby Dick Room; it looked a lot like a cheap rehabbed apartment, which it originally had been intended to be. The whole slam, inside and out, was painted an odd mustardy color which the paint store sold as "Colonial Gold," but which more closely resembled the shade of a slightly overcooked egg yolk. When this was pointed out to Vinnie, he pretended he'd done it on purpose.

In the older New Hampshire towns, the truth was only shared or volunteered. Those who had the audacity to ask for it deserved the prevarications, misdirections, and outright lies they received in answer. It was like a Code of the Northeast.

Everyone who was anyone or knew anyone in Dovekey Beach was sharing or volunteering what he or she knew at the B 'n' B that morning. Vinnie had to run to Shaw's Supermarket on Route 1 toward Hampton to buy more eggs and some of the bakery department's fantastic blueberry muffins, which he passed off as his own whenever anyone was vulgar enough to ask if they came out of his kitchen.

Vinnie thought he was ready for a good crowd, what with the meeting that had been called to discuss the gambling amendment some folks wanted added to the town charter. But he could not have planned for the especially hearty appetites that would develop with the news of Al Jenness's murder. The main dining room, the one with the foggy plate-glass picture window, reserved for nonsmokers and tourists (same thing if you asked him), was now filled with locals and heavy green-blue smog courtesy of R. J. Reynolds.

The lobstermen usually had their breakfasts just before dawn and then headed out to haul their traps. This morning all but the mavericks had set out to sea hungry so as to finish before the nine-thirty meeting.

Frank Will had set up among and yet apart from his contingent of political if not personal followers at the middle and far right of the main room. Jesse Kneeland had risen at three and made use of the full moon to finish his extensive line in time to join Frank, who had done the same. Avis Donigian had laid claim to the Moby Dick Room on behalf of her sister, who chose not to attend a public gathering while she smelled of rotting bluefish bait. Avis had also turned on the ceiling fan, despite the crisp morning, and requested that a no-smoking policy be honored in the pro-prostitution room. Frank was not the only person who laughed at the proscription, but since her room was closest to the door, the air stayed somewhat breathable.

The primary reason for the assembly might have been legislative, but the chatter was strictly prurient. No one expected Ruth

Jenness to show up the day after her husband had been found in such a compromising position—dead and all—but they had their hopes.

Especially Asa and Maggie Fleck, who thought they were going to expire with pent-up discretion until word of the homicide made its way naturally into the flow of the village. Given their superior inside information, the two volunteer paramedics did not even have to mingle. They sat on red plastic stools, side by side, at the short lunch counter and allowed the populace to come to them to be regaled with gory details. Maggie was already planning to write the book. She had decided on Sigourney Weaver to portray her in the movie. Asa thought Peggy Cass would be more appropriate, if she was still alive.

Frank sat at a table with Jesse, shoveling down a large stack of pancakes with real maple syrup and enjoying his neighbors' peripheral glances of deep-rooted suspicion nearly as much as his high-cholesterol meal. Jesse chain-smoked and fidgeted, but he did not want to get up and pace because it would have given the information-mongers a chance to get at him. Frank was his protection from prying. Frank never asked anyone a question he did not have a better answer to, so, rather than abuse themselves, potential interrogators avoided him like an IRS audit.

As much as he cared about Frank, Jesse was doggedly grateful that his Elizabeth was nothing like her father.

Except that she was exactly like him.

The ancient MGB sputtered and stalled on the road a hundred feet from the entrance to the B 'n' B. Used to automotive failure, Elizabeth opened the driver's door and, holding the steering wheel with her right hand and using old-fashioned leg power, steered the car onto the soft shoulder. She was freshly bathed, her hair still wet; she wore butter-soft deteriorating jeans, faded to powder blue from a thousand washings, a similar chambray shirt, and a dark gray leather bomber jacket. Through the sweating picture window,

Frank watched her expert parking maneuver and approach. She pulled the emergency brake and kicked the car door shut. Then she kicked it again.

"Ah. There she is," Frank announced from around a mouthful of pancake, "my daughter, the biker chick."

Jesse started to stand, decided against it and sat down, then stood back up by the time Elizabeth hit the glass door.

"Play hard to get, Jess," Frank advised. "But since you're up, can you get me another cup of coffee?" Mechanically, Jesse took Frank's heavy white Navy mug and edged his way through the Asa and Maggie fan club to the coffee machine.

Avis met her sister before she was three feet inside and led her into the smaller room. Several of the listeners at the counter took that as their cue to rejoin their political allies and reluctantly headed to the left side (apropos, Frank would say) of the building. The vote on the gambling issue was coming up in only one more day. Asa and Maggie would be spewing tales of horror for decades to come.

When Jesse returned with fresh coffee, Frank had finished eating and put his empty plate and cutlery on an adjoining table.

"She looks like she was crying, Frank. Was she crying this morning?" Jesse's eyes did not leave the door to the Moby Dick Room.

"Who?" Frank sipped at his black coffee.

"Liz," Jesse answered before he caught himself. He knew Frank was teasing him; he always did. But it was starting to make Jesse mad. "You know who I mean."

Frank pulled back a bit. "Yeah, I know. No, I don't think she was crying. I think she's just all scrubbed up. It's always made her a little pinkish." *Just like her mother,* he thought, and then stopped himself short. Elizabeth was not a baby anymore, and her mother could be turning just about any color under the sun these days, for all he knew.

"Maybe we should go in and find out what they're talkin' about," Jesse urged.

"Know what they're talkin' about," Frank answered. "Lizzie's goin' on and on about eminent domain, taking the islands that are most appropriate for Sin City and paying some pittance to the poor fools who've been payin' taxes on 'em for a thousand years so the rest of the carpetbaggers here onshore can pay a little bit less."

"Them scientists aren't paying no taxes," Jesse protested, unable to resist an opportunity to support Elizabeth, despite the fact that he hated the whole thought of turning the islands into some kind of Sodom and Gomorrah. Even though he knew better, Jesse had always thought of the islands as his own personal childhood fort. And he was not at all convinced that Elizabeth had *not* been crying. Everything Frank said was not true. It could not be that he was right 100 percent of the time.

Everyone was wrong sometimes. Even Frank.

Elizabeth finished her say to the gambling committee: eminent domain, lowering mainland taxes, her willingness to pick up the slack as best she could for the late Selectman Jenness.

Rollie Ouimet took the soapbox none too soon. Elizabeth's eyes were filled with tears again, whether from the smoke or her reference to Al as "late," she could not have said. As Elizabeth headed for the door, Avis asked if she was all right. Some fresh air would do her no harm, at least. Elizabeth mimed lighting a cigarette to her sister so she would not follow; Avis nodded, and Elizabeth made her escape to the exterior concrete step.

The air was warmer than the day before, the scent of nearby hyacinths carried in gusts. Suddenly Elizabeth wanted a cigarette to brutally smother such banal spring pleasures. The ubiquitous Jesse came unbidden to the rescue with a borrowed and lit Marlboro.

"You okay, Liz?" he asked, handing her the cigarette.

"How do I look, Jesse?" she snapped, but took the cigarette

anyway and immediately felt contrite. His attentions were actually very sweet. And who the hell did she think she was to reject him at every turn, just because he wasn't rich, brilliant, or, well, someone else? "Sorry, Jess. I need some sleep, that's all."

He did not believe her. He knew everything about the way Elizabeth Will could look. They had grown up together. He had seen her tired and rested, sick and healthy, at the top of a ski-team slope and at the bottom. He knew she had been crying all right.

And he knew Frank had lied to him again.

Ginny pulled the cruiser up behind Elizabeth's gallery. Frank's and Elizabeth's cars were both gone and she could hear Petunia's yipping from the house. Of course Elizabeth's MGB could just be in the shop; that was where it lived ninety percent of the time. Ginny had warned her buddy about double mufflers and hydraulic clutches, but it just made Elizabeth want the old clunker even more. She was a collector of lost causes—whether out of stubbornness or innate kindness, Ginny had never known for sure.

A knock on the gallery door got no answer, so Ginny walked back around to the rear of the building to look into the workshop area. Empty. Elizabeth and Frank must have finished their run early to make it back in time for the meeting at the B 'n' B. Neither one would miss the opportunity to cancel the other's vote.

But since she was already there, Ginny thought she should at least check at the house. Petunia was setting up a howl by then. She might need attention. Or so Ginny convinced herself.

Petunia was balanced on her hind legs with her water dish in her jowls, looking as pathetic as any tabloid picture of starving third world children. Ginny pushed at the peeling forest-green door, which swung in easily.

"Why, you poor sad thing, Petunia," she cooed, carrying the plastic dish to the sink. "Frank? Biz?" she called over the sound of running water. When the bowl was full, she carried it to the corner, where it was supposed to be kept to prevent early-morning bare-foot encounters. She kicked away Frank's pile of tools and head twine to make room. Petunia glanced at the dish happily and ran directly back to the counter. Ginny tried calling out one more time. "Biz, are you home? Frank?" Petunia scratched furiously at the face of the counter, tracing deep grooves worn in the soft wood by three generations of Will family cocker spaniels.

Ginny took a dog biscuit from the stoneware cookie jar and knelt down next to the slobbering dog. Petunia lapped long wet swaths up Ginny's face and stuck her velvety muzzle into Ginny's closed fist. Ginny kissed the dog's head and murmured, "You're a slut, Petunia, and I love you for it." She opened her hand and let the dog inhale the biscuit, chewing open-mouthed and enthusiastically flinging chunks a foot in every direction. Ginny closed the door behind her as Petunia snuffled the floor in search of edible debris. "Some watchdog," Ginny said, smiling to herself on the walk back to the cruiser, wondering whether or not to head straight to the Breakfast 'n' Beans to check out the action.

The concept of merely watching disgusted her, but she had found no direction for action. Spending hours of every day jaunting seven miles offshore to nose around was invigorating, to be sure, but aside from the start of a healthy tan it had netted her nothing. She needed a hook: one that would let Frank off his.

She leaned against the side of the police cruiser, crossed her arms, and frowned. Two orphaned lobster traps were thrown against the rear of the gallery, having somehow gotten separated from the haphazard stack in the front parking lot. Realizing how little she really knew about the industry that, along with the tourist trade, supported her town, she wandered over to take a closer look. *Not watching,* she reminded herself, *looking.*

Even with no commercial fishing experience, Ginny's eye caught a detail that made her stomach hitch and then sink as though it had been torpedoed.

"So, I talked to Bratter's Jewelry and they said it was no problem," Jesse told Elizabeth. "I'll stop by later to pick it up, drop it at the shop, and they said you can have it back in a coupla days." His eyes shone in eagerness. "It'd look wicked pretty on you, Liz. When I found it I was gonna have it done right t'way, but I wanted you to see it first."

The silver coin. Elizabeth's heart melted a bit toward Jesse. The world was turned upside down and he wanted her to look pretty. She wanted that, too. She also wanted Al Jenness to be alive. She wanted to believe her father had nothing to do with Al's death. Hell, she wanted her father to be normal and she wanted peace in the Mideast. And as kind as Jesse was, she didn't want to spend another evening with him.

"Jesse, look, I'm feeling kind of rotten today, probably a delayed reaction."

"I know, Lizzie, that's why I'll just stop by for a minute or two, maybe have a beer or two with Frank. You need some sleep, that's all. And in a coupla days you'll have your pirate treasure to hang around your neck."

Jesse had not called Elizabeth Lizzie since they were children playing house in the woods behind the backyard. It meant he was feeling possessive. Suddenly she was too tired to feel guilty anymore. When she looked over her shoulder and saw Frank loitering in the doorway of the Moby Dick Room, she became even more exhausted.

"Thanks, Jesse. Know what? Rollie Ouimet is talking right now, and you know how he goes on, so I've got a little time. Can I borrow the keys to your truck? I'll just pop home and bring the coin back with me before anything happens in there."

"I can drive you, Lizzie," Jesse offered. "Second gear can be something of a bitch if you don't know how to double-clutch."

"I *know* how to double-clutch," Elizabeth snapped and then

regrouped. "Dad taught me that before he taught me to parallel park. Don't you remember my mother yelling about us laying rubber all up and down the road in front of the house?" Jesse nodded and started to protest further, but Elizabeth cut him off. "And I could use a few minutes alone to think about the rest of the meeting, so can I borrow your keys?"

The house was no more than five minutes from the Breakfast 'n' Beans, Jesse calculated. He would lie in front of an oncoming train for Elizabeth, so the fact that he loved his truck almost as much as his boat, and that she had a lead foot that was legendary from Maine to Massachusetts, should not be *that* much of a factor. It was better than being splattered by the Amtrak Montrealer, anyway.

"Okay," he said, handing over his key ring. "But why don't I come along for the ride?"

She turned Jesse toward the door and pointed out Frank observing the meeting. "I'd really appreciate it if you'd make sure Dad doesn't start an international incident. You're the only person who could stop him."

Jesse doubted it, but was too flattered to say no.

"Okay." He nodded again. "But be careful of spitting up too much gravel. I just waxed her."

"I promise," she said. She patted his arm, and with immense relief got behind the wheel of the truck. Before turning over the engine, she shooed Jesse inside the B 'n' B.

She wished her car worked. She was pretty certain once she got home she wouldn't want to go back. *Isn't that always the way,* she thought, and wiped an errant tear from her cheek.

This was a perfect chance to try to locate something that had been missing since her mother moved out. Elizabeth had not dared ask Frank about it because it had been such a bone of contention between him and his wife. It had never seemed important enough before to dredge up old battles.

But something Ginny had said the night before had changed Elizabeth's mind.

Everything seemed to make her sad, lately.

The parlor heads on both the discarded traps had been slit. Both had been sloppily mended; one with polyester roping, the other with a soft cottony twine, both leaving an opening approximately seventeen inches in circumference. About the size of the neck of an adult male.

On momentum and instinct, Ginny Philbrick found herself marching directly into the musty darkness of the dilapidated barn behind the gallery after plucking the high-powered flashlight from the front seat of the cruiser.

A bare sixty-watt bulb dangled like a hanged man from a low rafter just inside the double doors, only one of which would open on its screaming hinges. The sooty chain pull had snapped three inches from the fixture sometime in distant history, and, tall as she was, Ginny had to stand on tiptoe to turn on the light. Even with the bulb illuminated, the arthritic fingers of light could not fold back the layers of voluminous blackness.

Cracks between the exterior boards splattered irregular slashes of daylight into the interior that were swallowed whole within an inch. Even sound was trapped in the thickness of dark scented cover. If birds sang, the song was caught and hung in the web of sodden ebony. The floor of rough-hewn native pine had sucked up generations of damp, buckling and rolling as would a ship's deck at sea. Huge hand-forged nails worked up here and there to tear the soles from shoes and remind the wearer not to shuffle around in shadowy places.

The beam of the flashlight made an incongruously modern slash in the dark. Dust motes floated like fairy dust through the intrusive artificial light.

This was a classic New England barn, left standing where

farms had gone the way of dinosaurs. There were rusted tools from the turn of the century, hung from spikes stuck willy-nilly into walls and rafters; rush-woven porch furniture turned squishy with age and humidity; a fabulously ornate pedestal table with mahogany veneer rippled like the pelt of a shar-pei puppy; box upon box of moldy *National Geographic* magazines; an unrepairable tricycle and two balloon-tire bicycles; lumber twisted into grotesque curves and shattered pieces waiting for a use yet undiscovered by humankind; skis, poles, skates, a toboggan; two birdcages with ancient yellow newspaper still lining the bottom; cases of canning jars worth a fortune on the flea market circuit; crippled and skewed picture frames empty or still sporting the faces of the long dead, watching Ginny accusingly; a turn-of-the-century floor safe weighing several hundred pounds, christened with potting soil and the broken bones of dozens of terra-cotta pots green with algae, spilling ancient powdering ledgers from its guts.

"Now what?" Ginny asked herself.

"How about explaining what you're doing here," Elizabeth Will answered from the doorway.

Jesse held fast, his sinewy forearms taut and ropey with the effort of restraining himself from causing grievous physical damage to the flailing French Canadian.

The two-man tussle had projected itself into the parking lot; the crowd, working hard to look horrified, but in fact having a bang-up time, followed. Inside, Frank went back to the counter to refill his coffee mug, all the while whistling "I Cain't Say No" from his favorite musical, *Oklahoma!*

Rollie Ouimet, exhausted by his own outrage, dropped toward the pavement like a tall and poorly filled sack of rags, but was held firm by Jesse. It took some time before the larger man realized he was holding back a functionally inanimate object. Rollie huffed feraciously to reoxygenate his lungs and recommence his spew of bilingual obscenities.

The onlookers quickly became bored, having heard the best Rollie had to offer back inside the Moby Dick Room, and wandered off to their cars, shaking heads and generally enjoying the beginning of a lovely late-spring day in New England.

"S'um of de bitch," Rollie gasped. "Dat by-gawd s'um bitch Frank Will. I someday him flatten, you betcha, by gawd der." He glared through the steamy picture window into the Breakfast 'n' Beans to see Frank tossing money and his check to the cashier. Rollie's wife, 350 pounds of womanhood and freshly coiffed raven hair, marched out of the restaurant and flung her husband's quilted jacket at him.

"You are pathetic, Roland," she said and walked to the robin's-egg-blue Ford pickup to wait for Rollie to pull himself together. The truth was, she was incredibly drawn to what she considered Rollie's passionate side and was now looking forward to making good use of the remainder of the morning, the afternoon, and probably most of the evening.

"She tink I be too small, you betcha, but I'm not cause I be fast," Rollie responded, slipping on his jacket and slapping Jesse on the back. "T'anks, Jess. Big Frank woulda by-gawd kilt old Rollie if I got to him, I tink. You be goot friend, der."

"Hey." Jesse shrugged off the compliment. He saw Avis, hands on hips, scowl on face, next to Frank inside. "Home safe, Rollie. See you at the Town Meeting."

"You betcha, by gawd," Rollie grumbled on his way to the passenger side of his truck. He slammed the door behind him.

The middle-aged waitresses were clearing the tables when Jesse returned. They were laughing raucously and dropping quarters along with the odd dollar bill into the calico aprons Vinnie insisted they wear on major occasions.

"You just couldn't resist, could you?" Avis asked her father under cover of the din of clattering plates and hilarity. "Rollie Ouimet doesn't have organized crime connections and you know it." Frank smiled satanically, infuriating Avis further. "You're just lucky Liz wasn't here, or your ass would be grass."

"Nice talk," Frank commented.

Avis was immediately contrite, first for having spoken to her father in such a way, and second for not having let her sister do the dirty work from beginning to end. Avis prided herself on being "the nice one."

"She's right," Jesse agreed, handing his waitress fifty cents and picking up his pouch of tobacco from the table where he and Frank had been sitting.

"Comments from the peanut gallery?" Frank said on his way to the exit and waved to Vinnie, who was taking nothing personally in the kitchen and waved back. "Shall we blow this pop stand?" Frank held the door open for Avis and Jesse. They waited for him to take the lead once again in the parking lot. Avis's Jeep was next to the door and she was in and buckling up before Jesse remembered that Elizabeth had absconded with his precious truck, leaving him like a beached whale in the company of Captain Ahab.

"Frank?"

"What, Jesse?" Frank pulled an enormous ring of keys from his broadcloth pants. The hilt of his thirty-eight was exposed in the waistband. Jesse thought it was a dangerous place to store a loaded pistol, but said nothing about it.

"Lizzie took my truck back to the house."

Frank opened the door to his truck. "Hop in."

Jesse shook his head and walked to the invalid MGB on the soft shoulder. The keys were in it. No reason to take them, he guessed. The sports car was undriveable without a good push or rebuilt everything.

"Think you can get behind her, here, and start me down the hill? If I pop the clutch I believe I can get her started."

"I'll do it," Avis offered. Jesse checked her front bumper—too high—and remembered how many times it had taken Avis to pass her driving test. And how many moving violations she had on her license.

"You can lead, Avis."

Frank's bumper was too high as well, but Jesse figured Frank could at least be counted on to hit the brakes rather than roll right over him and the tiny white car.

"Right!" Avis said, and started her engine, gunning the motor to an aviation-decibel roar.

Frank positioned himself at the door of Elizabeth's car for ease of advice-giving while Jesse tried to readjust the seat to accommodate his large frame.

"Hey, Frank?" Jesse asked as he fiddled underneath the seat, looking for the lever.

"It's on the left," Frank said.

"Will's Cottage *does* belong to you, doesn't it? Pop always said it did."

"Used to." Frank stuck his head in the car window and pulled the lever under the black bucket seat. Jesse shot back several inches. "My mother gave it up a long time ago."

Jesse wriggled into a more comfortable driving position and wondered if he dared ask the next question. He surprised himself.

"In 'thirty-nine?" Jesse pretended to examine the dashboard rather than look up at Frank for his reaction. Seconds passed in silence; Frank's shadow receded as he went back toward his own vehicle.

"Ayuh." Frank's answer carried on the breeze. The bashed-up truck's engine turned over. "Start her up, Jess. I'm comin' atcha."

Frank maneuvered quickly behind the MGB, and the two men followed as Avis took off with a spray of gravel, leaving them in the proverbial dust. The MGB's engine coughed into life, and Jesse and Frank were headed home.

Shame about Frank's sister, Jesse thought, listening intently for a hiccough from the MGB's motor. The girl was only eight years old when it happened. Sad. No doubt about it, 1939 was a bad year for the Wills. His pop always said Elizabeth was the spitting image: prettiest of the bunch.

No wonder Meg, Frank's mom, would never go back to Cap's Island.

Ginny stumbled over a box of papers. A swipe of the flashlight revealed a hodgepodge of yellowed pages, old books, and photostats. The cardboard container had not yet taken on the odor of the barn. She carried the box to the door where Elizabeth stood and turned back.

"Do you have a search warrant, Ginny?" Elizabeth said. With the light behind her and her hands on her hips, she looked like an old Wonder Woman comic panel. Ginny was not in the mood to appreciate the melodramatic stance.

"Nope." She riffled through a stack of framed photographs taken as far back as the mid-1800s and poorly executed oil paintings from the 1950s that leaned against a near wall. Tucked here and there were also sundry documents and awards, including Elizabeth's penmanship certificate from the eighth grade. Ginny remembered the presentation ceremony as though it had happened that week. *How time marches on.*

"Then I think you'd better go roust Judge Spirou and get yourself something that gives you the right to poke around."

One particular photograph caught Ginny's eye. It was of a fragile old woman standing somberly in an English-style garden. Wind had released a strand of hair from the stiff salt-and-pepper pile on top of the woman's head and had it gesturing in the direction of some construction project in the background. Men, tiny in the distance, hung from wooden scaffolding, captured loafing forever. Choppy water lay to the woman's right. The neck of her linen blouse rose high and was ornamented by a Victorian brooch. The photo had been enlarged to eleven by fourteen inches, and the old woman's dark eyes stared directly into Ginny's. Familiar. Ginny lifted the frame and laid it across the cardboard box she had set aside.

"There's something I have to show you, Biz," Ginny said.

"I've seen everything there is in this damned barn, Ginny. A thousand times. So have you."

"I don't think you have," Ginny answered. "But what I have to show you isn't in the barn." She stepped past Elizabeth and into the dappled shade of the yard. Elizabeth followed her the twenty feet to the rear of the gallery. Ginny stooped, reaching into her pocket. She pulled out the Swiss Army knife Frank had given her for her Sweet Sixteen birthday. The copy of Al Jenness's note fell to the ground. Ginny cursed her memory lapse. "Do you know anything about these? Ruth Jenness had a note in her hand with your name and then this series of numbers, written by Al, the morning you found his body."

"What did Ruth say about it?" Elizabeth asked and took the paper for a closer look.

"She was grieving at that moment. She didn't say anything."

"Well, I don't have a clue what these numbers mean. It's not a telephone number; there's one digit too many. The numbers go too high for the state lottery. I don't know, Ginny. Are you sure that was all Al wrote?" Ginny thought she heard an odd eagerness in her friend's voice.

"I'm sure," Ginny affirmed and released a short, wickedly sharp blade from the assortment within the pocket knife. "See these?" She gestured downward.

"They're lobster pots," Elizabeth answered dryly. "I guess the hell I've seen them. I've mended enough of them in my day."

Ginny's throat constricted. She was too close to all of this; way too close.

"You mend these, Biz?"

Elizabeth's face became a wall of composure. She joined Ginny, kneeling beside the two traps and inspecting them. The square knots tied in the mismatched twine jumped out from the symmetry of the knitted heads and marked the gashes in the netting distinctly.

"I don't remember," Elizabeth answered quietly.

"I think you do, Biz. I don't think you knew anything about these two traps until I asked." Ginny cut a small sample of the mending string from each trap and placed the pieces in the pocket of her uniform pants.

They heard slamming noises outside the barn and for a second Elizabeth thought it was her heart whacking in a frenzy to escape her ribcage.

A shadow fell across their backs. Elizabeth, startled, lost her balance and fell to the ground on one hip. Ginny stood and held out her hand to her best friend. Elizabeth took it, though it was not necessary. Adrenaline alone could have lifted and carried her to the shoals and back.

"I was just saying"—Elizabeth punctuated each word, angry at Ginny, herself, and the world—"that I don't remember who mended these pots."

"Shit, Liz," Frank said with a smile, "I did. 'Tweren't that damned dog up at the house."

"Thanks, Frank," Ginny said. "I thought so."

Avis and Jesse crowded into the doorway. They both expelled air as though they had been kicked in the midsection.

"Jeez, Frank," Jesse muttered sadly. Frank smiled innocently and raised an eyebrow.

"It was an experiment," he explained without seeming to care whether or not anyone believed him. "Pretty simple."

"Not so simple, I'm afraid. I'm going to have to take them, Frank," Ginny responded.

"Gonna knit me some new heads, Gin?" Frank crossed his arms and leaned against the gallery siding.

"Wish I could, Frank. I'm taking a box of stuff out of the outbuilding, too."

"You got a search warrant?" Jesse asked, slow on the uptake but sincere as all get-out.

"Doesn't need one, Jess," Frank answered. He nodded to Ginny. "Sure, go ahead. Been meaning to clean the place out any-way."

Avis pulled her eyes away from the damning lobster traps, afraid.

"What are you looking for, Gin? Those traps aren't evidence, except circumstantial. You know how Dad's always fiddling around with stuff. Everyone knows that."

"That's right," Jesse agreed.

Ginny stacked the pots and lifted them easily. The wood was porous from several seasons immersed in salt water, sucked dry as dust. Without the brick ballasts, the pots weighed less than two bags of groceries. Frank opened the back door of the police cruiser so Ginny could load them. The trunk would have been too small. Ginny nodded her thanks and went back into the barn to take the box of papers and the photograph. Frank's daughters stood mute. Ginny opened the trunk of her car and loaded in the last haul.

"Thanks, Frank," Ginny said. She turned to the others. "You guys know the drill."

"Don't leave town," Frank filled in, pleased with himself. Ginny nodded without pleasure. She jotted Al Jenness's cryptic numbers on the back of a moving violation form and handed it through the window to Elizabeth.

"Let me know if any of these numbers mean anything to you. And I don't want to find any one of you setting foot on the islands for a while, either," she finished. The car door slammed. Jaw set,

Ginny drove off, wishing she could keep going until she saw the sterile, objective spire of the Empire State Building.

"What's out there, Dad?" Elizabeth asked.

"Where?" Frank pulled the chain on the barn light and closed the double doors.

"You know where. The isles. What's out there?"

"Nothing," Frank grunted and slammed the padlock that had never worked through the aluminum ring on the building doors. "Never been nothing out there for us." He faced the three people in the world who really cared about him and added, "And I catch you out there, there's gonna be hell to pay, you better believe it."

"We have traps to haul out there," Elizabeth protested.

"And we'll haul them, but we got no business anymore walking on those godforsaken shit piles, you hear me?" There was no response. "You *hear* me?" Avis nodded, Jesse stood wide-eyed, and Elizabeth shot daggers with her green eyes, refusing to move any part of her body in any way that could be interpreted as agreement. Her father stood firm for almost a minute, neither he nor Elizabeth so much as blinking.

Then, with a courtly inclination of his head, Frank eased his way out of the little group and toward the house. "I'm taking a nap now. All this excitement has me dead on my feet."

Dead on my feet.

Dead tired.

Dead to the world.

Dead in the water.

Dead end.

Elizabeth snuffed a small amused sound at the expense of the English language.

There was nothing else left to laugh at and she had already had her cry for the year.

FOURTEEN

ALL HELL WAS breaking loose in Garrett Selby's sanctuary. The perfectly maintained parquet floor was pimpled with balled-up wads of paper. Stacks of books balanced helter-skelter among the rubble, the empty shelves where they belonged incongruous and disturbing as a plucked eye socket.

"How could you *not* have seen anything?" Garrett Selby ranted at his brother. "You live at that end of the island. It's not as though there are hordes of people storming all over out here."

"Well, as commanded, I didn't see anything or anyone," Eli answered with a salute from where he sat at the end of the room. "And"—he moved the wingback chair slightly to catch more of the sunlight—"I'm not *in* the cottage twenty-four hours a day. Also by your command, if I remember." Eli kept his voice moderate, though he wanted to bellow until the walls shook. Mandatory prayer with the congregation four times a day, indeed. A complete waste of his time—and God's if there was one. "What about your followers? How many are out here right now, anyway? Everyone in Bellevue, or just selected wings?"

The reverend was on his hands and knees sifting through documents, careful not to break the back of the old portfolio in which they had been stored. He ignored his younger brother's acerbic characterization of his transitory parishioners.

"My congregation has strict orders to avoid that side of the island. The collapsed buildings make the entire area too dangerous."

"What about me?" Eli asked bitterly.

"You too," Garrett answered, not explaining whether he meant that the ruins were too dangerous or his brother's heretical leanings were. In any event, his people obeyed him. Always. The broken garden trowel he had found in the forbidden area could not belong to any member of his congregation, and his brother had no reason to lie to him about it, either. Someone—an off-islander— had been digging around Garrett Selby's holy preserve and, by God, would pay for it.

"What are you looking for?" Eli asked impatiently. He wanted to nap a bit and catch up on some missed sleep. Though ten years younger than Garrett, he was looking the same age. Eli found that disheartening. He meant to get back to Boston someday and would prefer to look presentable.

"A 1920 chart of the island."

"Well, I can certainly see why that's of utmost importance at this minute." Eli yawned.

"It is if we want to catch our intruder." Garrett carefully replaced the chart at which he was looking and picked up another. Eli could not have cared less and would have said so if he had had the energy. "Ah," Garrett piped, "here it is." He stood up, giving a small grunt. "Let's go."

"Where?" Eli asked. "There's no place *to* go on this damned island."

"Watch your language, Eli. It's just that kind of sloppy morality that put you behind bars in the first place."

And here in the second place, Eli thought to himself.

Garrett continued. "If you don't mend your ways and see the

light of righteousness you will be doomed, yes doomed, to live in sin for the rest of your miserable days."

Eli sincerely hoped his brother was right on that score.

Sweat glistened and ran rivers down Charles MacKay's back and arms. The weight burned his muscles; the bar made an angry red mark across his chest on every repetition. One more. He was still filled with kinetic energy despite what would have been a murderous day for most men. After so many hours on the water, he was exhilarated rather than exhausted.

He dropped to the floor. He counted push-ups, hoping the monotony would soothe him.

At 100, he realized he could not be soothed. At least not through exercise.

"Dig here," Garrett Selby commanded his brother, who was dozing at the base of an obelisk carved with faded letters and a voluptuous cherub. Garrett kicked away several charred bricks. He double-checked the urine-yellow paper and reassured himself that they were in the correct spot. "Eli!"

Eli stood and brushed rusty dried moss from his slacks. A tennis sweater was tied over his shoulders in case the day should cool off. He wished he had brought gloves to protect his hands from any adverse cosmetic effects of shoveling. Shattered glass twinkled beneath his feet, becoming more profuse as he approached his brother, whom he joined on a three-foot swell of rubble. A small green talc can peeked up from behind a stand of sea grass. Eli picked it up and tucked it in a back pocket. A souvenir for the day he could look back on his enforced vacation on the island and laugh.

"Before I raise a sweat, do you mind telling me what's been going on around here lately? It's too early for the kind of water traffic we've been getting, and I couldn't help but notice the cop making a house call. You told the board that this place was isolated from the mainland."

"It is, and will stay that way." Eli looked dubious. "Well, there *has* been talk about turning these shoals into a haven for gambling and prostitution. A shortsighted tax plan that will surely lead—"

"No shit," Eli interrupted.

"Eli . . . ," Garrett warned.

"You mean they're going to take your little pre-apple Eden and convert it into a fruit salad of sin? That is *too* good."

"They cannot touch this island," Garrett insisted. "The rights to this land were sold to the Episcopal Church in 1880. We bought the hotel from them in 1942. There is no precedent for taking church land by eminent domain. No precedent at all, ever. I researched it extensively. The library here contains the most complete historical and legal documents regarding these islands in the world." Garrett's voice gained intensity. "No one will usurp us for any reason. Do you understand? Do you understand that, Eli? God is on our side." Spittle formed at the sides of the preacher's mouth.

"Oh, I understand," Eli said, humoring Garrett. He understood the ins and outs of bookies, oddsmakers, and hookers far better than did his older, weirder brother. And Eli's checkered past had acquainted him more thoroughly with the judicial system as well. Eli might never have a place in heaven, but with a little planning and luck he might be able to treat himself to a more luxurious pad while he was waiting for his eternal flop in hell. He promised to have a look at those records himself, and changed the subject. "What did this mess I'm digging used to be, anyway?"

Garrett answered automatically, his mind elsewhere. "Domestics' quarters and another hotel built here during the tourist heyday."

"What happened? This must have been some complex."

"Struck by lightning and burned to the ground." Garrett

pointed to the area he wanted dug. "Here. Lightning was God's will."

Eli thought it might have been an accident of nature but was not in the mood for a theological discussion.

"What are we looking for, anyway?"

"A freshwater well. According to this chart, it should be right around here."

"May I ask why we're, excuse my use of the word, divining?" Eli leaned on his shovel. "If you're thirsty, I'd be more than happy to hit the mainland and pick up a couple of six-packs."

"Ah"—Garrett sighed patiently—"but that would be a violation of your parole, wouldn't it?" Eli rammed the shovel's blade into the debris. "No, my brother, we are going to bait a trap." Eli stopped mid-shovel.

"You mean, set some poor fool up to fall into a deserted well? If the fall didn't kill him, then drowning would. Forget it, brother, I'm a lot of things but I'm not a murderer." He waited for Garrett to come to his senses and agree. He did not. "Who do you think you are, anyway, God?"

"No, Eli, I'm not. But I am my brother's keeper, and you'd better remember that."

Eli's shovel struck something hard. Chewing on Garrett's statement, he dug down into the shards and came up with a piece of statuary. It was the white marble sculpture of a child's hand.

Frank Will went to the room he had shared for thirty-five years with his wife, Sal, and refused to come out. For an hour Elizabeth and Avis bickered with the kind of ferocity they had not displayed since Elizabeth had turned thirteen and called off the war of the Wills. That had been only fair, since it had always been Elizabeth who instigated sibling troubles.

"We have to ask him," Avis insisted.

"He'll only lie," Elizabeth said. "If he had something to do with Al's murder, he can't tell us. If he didn't, he'll feel he's lost some of his patina of danger and get his nose out of joint because we questioned his questionable integrity. It's lose-lose. I'm not playing."

"This is out of hand now, Liz. We have to ask."

"Oh no you don't. Don't use the word 'we' when you mean 'me.' You do what you want and count me out of it."

The two women went around and around. They heard Frank in the first-floor bedroom. Periodically their arguing was drowned out by the sound of furniture moving and they stopped to listen. Several times Avis marched to the door, stopped, shook her head, and returned to fight with Elizabeth rather than face her father.

Avis made Western sandwiches with extra onions, hoping the aroma would coax Frank from his lair. It didn't work. Petunia ate the leftovers and then scratched at Frank's door to get away from the hostilities in the kitchen.

"You're such a chicken-shit, Avis."

"Am not."

"Are so."

"Prove it." Avis slammed the refrigerator door, inspiring furious scratching from Petunia. Neither woman saw the bedroom door open a crack to let the dog in.

"You have been dying to ask about Al and me for months," Elizabeth snapped. "It's been killing you since we all started working on the new legislation. You couldn't even ask your own sister about a little adultery in the state that brought America *Peyton Place*. You"—she threw her dirty dish in the sink, breaking two glasses at the same time—"are a chicken-shit."

"So, were you?" Avis busied herself cleaning glass out of the sink, suddenly not wanting to know any secrets from anyone. She was beginning to believe that spending two weeks with Gerald's parents would have been more pleasant than staying home.

"Ask the whole question, if you want to know. Was I what, Avis? What?"

"Were you and Al Jenness having an affair." Once it was said, Avis went on a binge. "Were the two of you sleeping together, committing adultery, bumping uglies? *Were* you? My God, Liz, it makes a difference. I have to know how sorry I have to feel for all of us, here, not just Dad."

"Feel better?"

"I will when I get an answer." Avis crossed her arms and leaned back against the sink.

Elizabeth studied her younger sister and seemed to struggle with herself for a moment, mouth opening to answer and then shutting again. Finally she said, "That's none of your business."

"Dammit, Liz!" Avis shouted, smacking the palms of her hands against the kitchen counter.

"Goes double for me," Frank said from the bedroom doorway, Petunia cowering behind his legs. He slapped his cowboy hat on his head and led the dog between his two daughters. "I'll be in the barn sorting if you need me to break anything up," he said and left, the spaniel scrabbling between his legs to get away as fast as possible.

"I'm going to my room," Avis said sulkily, taking a liter of Diet Pepsi with her.

Elizabeth kicked the dog's water dish, spraying liquid from one end of the kitchen to the other. She went to the walk-in pantry, where she threw unbreakables about until she located an undoubtedly stale carton of Newports her mother had left on her last visit at Christmas.

The gold bracelet Al had given her for her birthday glittered on her wrist when she lit up. The smoke tore a path down her throat, and she enjoyed her own discomfort. It *was* none of sister's business, though there were times she ached to talk about her relationship with Jenness. It seemed to Elizabeth that sometimes her life was nothing but one expanding and retracting ache.

And she had a one-woman show opening in less than a week. Shoving a crumpled pack of cigarettes into the pocket of her jeans, she marched down to the gallery to frame some show-quality pieces she had, mercifully, completed before the murder had hit the fan.

Her father was tossing things around in the barn. Every once in a while she heard glass and wood splintering. Several times she saw him lugging huge plastic bags of refuse to the side of the road for the garbage collectors to pick up later in the week. She wondered what Ginny Philbrick would think of this sudden attack of fastidiousness on the part of Big Frank Will.

It had taken the ruination of a very expensive pair of wool slacks and two broken nails, but Ruth Jenness located what she was looking for taped to the bottom of one of Al's six-foot filing cabinets at the rear of the office. She had emptied each drawer before she lost her temper and tossed the cabinet on its side. Her ultimate success made her rethink all those years of steely self-control.

Betty had been given the day off, and Ruth had hung a Closed sign on the door before the search began. The custom-ordered diaphanous pleated shade (light federal blue) was drawn down over the large front window, but still allowed light to enter. Though her car was parked in its space by the door, Ruth was confident that her neighbors would not intrude on her grief.

Using an already jagged fingernail, she slit open the nine-by-eleven unmarked manila envelope and pulled out a short stack of papers. As she examined an original lease agreement dated 1880, the blue back fell into her lap. Folded into thirds, the cover was printed with the name of Spirou and Vennard, Attorneys, and an address in Concord.

She opened the papers with a feeling of contentment. The

blue back held a draft for approval of divorce proceedings to be instituted at a date to be determined by the Plaintiff (Al) at a later time. Ruth smiled. She dropped the extraneous documents onto Al's desk, replaced the legal papers and a small three-by-five-inch piece of notepaper in the larger mailing envelope, and taped it where it had been at the bottom of the last drawer.

Vindication. For all the denials and counterclaims, Ruth had the proof she had been looking for. Al Jenness and Elizabeth Will had been having an affair. Ruth chuckled, pleased at how right she had been all along. It took more than an hour for her to straighten out the work scattered over the floor and return it to the repositioned file, but she was happy with the use of her afternoon.

Her husband was an adulterer. So what?

He was dead, and she was more alive than she had been in twenty years.

After a quick trip to the house, Frank returned to the barn with the dog. Man and best friend entered the gallery in a cloud of must and dust. Petunia sneezed twice as Frank placed the wooden crate filled with empty picture frames on the carpeted floor.

"Gesundheit," Elizabeth and Frank said to the spaniel in unison.

"Thought you could use some of these old frames," Frank said. "Barn's too damp to keep pictures, no room at the house, so I took them out."

"Good idea," Elizabeth answered warily.

"That's what I thought," Frank said. He took a beer from the small refrigerator and offered one to her. She shook her head. Neither knew what to say, so they considered it something of a blessing to hear the entrance door open. Ginny Philbrick's voice cut the moment short.

"Biz? You in back?"

"I'm here, Ginny. So is Dad."

Ginny walked directly into the back room. "Is Avis up at the house?" she asked. "We need to have a talk."

Elizabeth locked the gallery door, and the threesome were inside the kitchen within five minutes. Avis returned from her walk in the woods shortly thereafter, wearing a concerned look. Ginny wasted no time getting to the crux of the matter.

"I want to talk to Sal. Where's your mother, Elizabeth?"

"No need to bother Sal," Frank drawled. "She'll only raise a hissy fit and start blaming me for getting into trouble."

"You *are* in trouble, Frank," said Ginny. "Avis, how can I contact your mother?"

"She's not going to want to come up from Boston, Gin, but I'll call her on the phone and you can talk to her if that's good enough."

"It would be, Avis, but I've been calling your mother for two days now and her answering machine keeps picking up. I got ahold of her landlady; she told me your mother disappeared about a week ago without a word."

"Dad?" Elizabeth and Avis asked simultaneously.

"Beer?" he offered Ginny in response.

"Wait a minute," said Elizabeth, "I got a letter from her a couple of weeks ago. I didn't read it all that carefully because she printed it out on that damned dot matrix printer of hers in a type-face so small it was giving me a headache." Elizabeth continued talking as she climbed the stairs to the second floor, where her room and Avis's were. Her voice was diminished by distance, but still clear. "She probably told me she was leaving town for some writing convention or other; I don't even pay attention any more, she spends so much time traveli—"

"Find it?" Avis yelled up the stairs. There was no answer. "Liz, did you *find* it?" There was a muffled word in response. *"Liz? We can't hear YOU."*

"Ginny?" Elizabeth called. "Philbrick," she shouted with more strength, "get your ass upstairs, okay?"

Ginny bolted up the stairs two at a time, Frank behind her, Petunia behind him, Avis bringing up the rear. Elizabeth was standing in her bedroom doorway and pushed the paneled door wide open when they were all crowded behind her.

Laid in the center of the white down comforter on Elizabeth's bed were the crucified remains of a large seagull. Aviary mites swarmed around the carcass like blackheads on white skin.

The only sound in the room was of Elizabeth's frantic breathing, rapid as a machine gun.

FIFTEEN

THE DEAD SEAGULL, along with its slatwork crucifix, had been bagged and hidden away in the trunk of the police cruiser parked in the driveway. Ginny Philbrick was now the proud owner of two crucified birds, official custodian of one murdered public official, and reluctant bodyguard to a very suspicious bunch of old family friends. And Avis was driving her stark, staring nuts.

The younger Will sister was baking brown-sugar brownies while she and Ginny waited for the doctor to come downstairs after tending to Elizabeth in Avis's room. The men had carried Elizabeth across the hall after she fainted. *Fainted,* Avis mused. Her big sister keeled over like a giant dandelion in the path of a Weed Whacker.

Hyperventilation, Dr. Ryan said, and shooed everyone from the room. When Frank and Jesse would not leave, he sent them both to the corner store to pick up some Benadryl. It wouldn't do Elizabeth or anyone else any good until one of them caught a cold or hay fever season hit, but it got the men out from underfoot.

"She's sleeping," Ryan commented as he entered the kitchen and sniffed the air. "Brown-sugar brownies?" he asked, after one sniff. "How long till they come out of the oven?"

"Five minutes," Avis answered.

"Good," Ryan said, tapping a cigarette from the pack in his sport coat pocket. "I can wait."

"Biz going to be okay?" Ginny asked, flipping open her Zippo and lighting the doctor's Lucky.

"Physically, right as rain once the drugs wear off. I shot her up with enough Valium to fell a professional wrestler." He shook his head in wonder. "The whole family has this elephant tolerance for pharmaceuticals."

Avis opened the oven door to check on the brownies. "None of us has ever done drugs."

"Good thing," Ryan said wryly. "Couldn't a one of you afford a dosage high enough to get a buzz. Got any coffee there, Avis?"

"I can make some."

Elizabeth's letter from their mother said nothing about a trip anywhere, so Sal was definitely missing. Avis would have organized a barn-raising for the doctor to keep her mind busy.

"Let's see if I can find a can," Avis said, and disappeared into the walk-in pantry. Ginny reached into her pants pocket and pulled out what looked to Ryan very much like a small ball of lint.

"This look familiar, Doc?" Ginny asked, exposing two short sections of twine in the flat of her hand. The old man slipped a pair of bifocals onto his nose and peered down.

"That's not the question you're asking me, Ginny. You're asking me if either of these samples matches the twine that knotted Al Jenness into that lobster trap. Ayuh?"

"Ayuh."

The sounds of boxes and canned goods being rearranged came through the wall from the pantry. Ginny knew Elizabeth kept the coffee in the refrigerator, but was not about to direct Avis, since she wanted some time alone with the doctor.

"Don't know," Ryan answered Ginny. "One of them looks close, but you'll need the lab in Concord to confirm it." He got up, grabbed a pot holder, and removed the brownies from the oven. There was a sound from the floor above of an overweight cocker spaniel jumping off a bed; then they heard her trotting downstairs. Ryan placed the pan on top of the stove, next to which Petunia stationed herself.

"Wait a minute." Ginny stood and walked over to the area next to the dog's water. "I saw some more roping right here the other night." The coil of twine was gone. "Damn. Frank must have put it away."

"Listen to yourself," Ryan chastised. "Frank has never, in my lifetime, put anything away where it belongs. Liz must have done it."

"Yeah, you're right," Ginny agreed. "I'll ask her about it when she comes to."

"Tomorrow."

"Yeah, tomorrow. By the way, Doc, the official coroner confirmed your autopsy findings."

"What?" Avis shouted from the pantry.

"Nothing, Avis." Ginny lowered her voice. "Al died of a massive coronary following a cerebral hemorrhage, possibly, though not definitely, exacerbated by a blow to the head."

"No fear of drowning in that damned pot, then."

"They say not. He was dead as a mackerel before he was bound in."

"Well, that's something, anyway. I suppose you'll want me to be sending those samples to Concord for matching." Ginny nodded and handed them over. Ryan stubbed out his cigarette and immediately lit another. "Got any idea who planted the gull in Elizabeth's room?"

"I first suspected Frank, until I looked at his face. I don't think I've ever seen him so quiet—and helpless."

"Probably his silence got him confused. Hard to believe a stranger carrying road kill could have snuck in by a family dog, though." Ryan exhaled. Petunia's attention was fixed on the out-of-reach pan of brownies. Ginny and Ryan shrugged at each other, dismissing the protective dog argument. Avis came back into the kitchen holding a can of LaTourraine coffee aloft like a basketball trophy.

"Found it!"

Ryan shook his head. "They haven't made LaTourraine in about a kazillion years, Avis. Why don't you check the refrigerator for a more contemporary brand?"

"I gotta get going," Ginny apologized. "Avis, tell your sister I'll be by to see her tomorrow, okay? Think you can spend the night?"

"Sure."

"And if you hear from your mother, give me a call. Day or night. Understand?" Ryan took the coffee canister from the freezer, measured the proper amount for a full pot into the filter, added water to the machine, and turned it on.

"You don't think anything's happened to her, do you, Gin?" Avis's forehead was crinkled, her mouth slightly open.

"Don't know, Avis. Hope not."

Frank and Jesse rattled back shortly thereafter with three different packages of Benadryl, for which the doctor thanked them profusely. They all had several brownies and too many cups of coffee before Jesse and Ryan took their leave. Frank paced until Avis thought she'd slap him out of sheer caffeine nerve. Hanging onto her "niceness" with white knuckles, she did not, of course.

As Elizabeth slept, Avis tried to divert herself with television, but Frank continued to travel in wandering circles with Petunia at his heels, back and forth in front of the screen, until Avis shut off the noise and picked up an old *Analog* pulp from a pile next to Frank's recliner.

"I can't sleep," Frank announced unnecessarily.

"I told you that you ought to switch to decaf, but no one

listens to me," Avis responded testily, tossed the sci-fi magazine aside and picked up an *Aviation* from the carpet. "We'll probably all be up all night now."

"Maybe Jesse's up for a game of chess."

"Great idea. You go. Elizabeth's going to be out of it until morning."

"Think?"

"Dr. Ryan said so."

"Well, then, I guess I'll go visit Jesse. You can call there if you need me for anything."

"Thanks, Dad. Go."

"Okay. I'm going."

"Bye." Frank grabbed his quilted jacket off the floor and started out of the living room. Petunia looked up briefly from the brownie she had stolen off the kitchen table and went back to chewing.

"Oh, Dad?"

"What?"

"Do we have any chamomile tea?"

Frank examined his daughter for signs of instability. "You're kidding, right?" He left.

Sandy's studio was aglare with fluorescent light. The work table was covered with an old sheet, a faded floral percale laid out like a banquet with the remains of the two battered seagulls, still nailed to their jagged boards. Both Ginny and Sandy were holding glasses of red wine, though only Ginny appeared to be drinking any.

"Notice anything, Sandy?"

"Besides the bugs crawling all over my worktable?"

"Between the two carcasses. You're the artist. What's the difference between the two of them?"

Sandy stood beside Ginny and leaned over the table for a better look. She did not *want* a better look, but did want to support

Ginny. The gulls were different sizes but, as far as Sandy could tell, the same species. She wondered whether she was supposed to be able to tell whether they were different sexes, and decided that probably only gulls knew such things. The boards to which the birds were nailed were of different varieties, one set driftwood, the other scrap lathing, but that was so obvious she was sure Ginny was not asking about that. As a worker in clay, stone, and metal, Sandy didn't think about color that much, so it took her a moment to realize what Ginny might be referring to.

"The bigger gull is splattered with blood. The smaller one has just a small black hole. Right?"

Ginny smiled. "Right. And?" she prompted.

"And so the birds died in different ways. The big one slowly, splattering blood all over the place; the small one quickly by an arrow or a rock or—"

"A gunshot." Ginny nodded to herself. With a narrow finishing chisel, she dug through the single hole in the smaller gull's breast; the blunt end of the chisel hit wood. The hole went directly through. "Larger caliber than a twenty-two. Probably a thirty-eight. What else, Sandy?"

"I don't *know.*" Sandy slugged down a mouthful of wine. "Different nails. The bloody gull is attached by big aluminum ones and the little one with"—she leaned closer—"littler copper ones?"

"Right." The kind of nails used in good-quality lobster pots to resist corrosion in the water, Ginny thought but did not say. "And," she continued, "the big gull was crucified alive, and the other was dead—but dead some time, I'd say by the desiccation of the body. Still"—Ginny was just talking now, to herself more than to Sandy—"even though this smaller gull has been dead for weeks, no other birds have been lunching on it. I wonder why? Did somebody *save* the body just in case? Unlikely," she answered herself. "Where could it have been to deteriorate without being cannibalized by other gulls?"

Sandy had no answer to that one. She watched Ginny rebag the evidence and chew on her bottom lip.

"Let's go watch Letterman, Gin. It'll come to you the minute you stop thinking about it."

Ginny was doubtful, but did not want to miss the Top Ten List. Maybe the subject for that night would be the top ten reasons Frank Will could not have killed Al Jenness. Ginny did not have one.

The peeling Cape Cod house was achingly silent except for the periodic chiming of the antique Seth Thomas mantel clock and the *chnnnng hmmmm* of the old Frigidaire turning itself on and off in the kitchen. Channel 38 out of Boston was airing a classic Christopher Lee vampire movie produced by J. Arthur Rank—the kind that scared Avis to death but that she could not resist watching. Elizabeth used to force her to watch when they were small, and now it was a noxious habit.

Christopher Lee bent over the neck of the lovely pale actress with the teased hair and white lipstick. He whispered something Avis could not quite make out, so she turned up the volume on the remote control just a hair and leaned forward on the sofa, scrinching her eyes on the off chance it would make her hear more clearly. It did not. Eyes locked on the screen, she reached for the remote control once more. Ominous shadows crept forward in the gloom behind Christopher Lee, the actress arched her swan neck, and . . .

"Aaaavisssssssssssss."

"What!" The remote flew from Avis's hand and clattered across the coffee table; her other fist clutched the homemade multi-paned afghan for protection. Elizabeth slumped on the sofa next to her sister.

"What time is it? I feel like crap."

Avis smacked her with a small sofa cushion. "I *hate* you."

"Yeah, well," Elizabeth commented offhandedly. "What time is it?"

"You're supposed to be asleep," Avis accused, looking at the mantel clock. "It's almost one in the morning."

"Yeah, well," Elizabeth repeated. "Everyone gone?"

"Yeah. Go back to bed." Avis retrieved the remote control from the floor and started channel surfing. She did not have the intestinal fortitude for a Rank movie tonight. Something along the lines of an infomercial—even spray-painting Ron Popeil—would be less nerve-wracking.

"Dad's out, too?" Elizabeth asked, taking the remote and re-setting it to Channel 38. Christopher Lee's face filled the screen, blood dripping from his mouth onto the impressive breast of his victim.

"He went over to Jesse's. We had an awful lot of coffee, so everyone—except you, supposedly—is wide awake."

"Good. There's something I want to check out in Dad's room."

"No, there isn't. Go back to bed."

"Yes, there is. You coming?"

"No." Avis thought for a second. "Is this important?"

"I think so. It has to do with Mom."

"I'm coming." Avis grunted and got up off the couch. "I'm coming."

Frank and Sal's room was on the first floor, toward the woods, in a nineteenth-century addition just off the living room. Neither of the sisters had been in the room for years. Frank threw his linens and dirty clothes in a plastic laundry basket and carted them to the basement himself for washing. The door was always kept closed, Elizabeth assumed because Frank was not a bed maker by nature and keeping his rubble out of sight was his concession to her nag-ging about living like humans.

The bedroom door mechanism made an unnaturally loud

click in the quiet of the old house. Avis looked behind her and toward an ominous shuffling sound. As it approached, she grabbed her sister's arm in a pincer grip.

Petunia, stupider than usual from sleep, wandered to her side. "What if Dad comes home?" Avis asked.

"Petunia will throw herself at the door the way she always does at the first sound of his truck. Now let go of my arm." Elizabeth shook off her sister's grasp and swabbed the wall just inside the door, feeling for the light switch. On her third try she hit it, but the room remained dark. "Wonder what year the overhead bulbs burned out," she groused and groped her way to the nearest nightstand lamp. Carefully she fingered her way downward from the shade and located the switch. "Jeez." She grimaced into the harsh light. "Does Dad always have to use hundred-watt bulbs?"

The room had not been repainted or redecorated in the eleven years since Sal had moved to Boston. The walls remained a virulent Pepto-Bismol pink; dust webs hung like Spanish moss from the pastel wallpaper border just below the ceiling. Pale pink chiffon sheers fainted limply from between heavy floral swags. The burgundy shag carpet lay beaten and defeated beneath their feet. Grandmother Meg's pre-Depression bedroom suite of dark mahogany stood heavily where it had been placed before either of the daughters had been born. Petunia jumped into the center of the rumpled bed and commenced a well-deserved nap. Elizabeth went immediately to the nightstand by the side of the four-poster pineapple bed that had been her mother's and slid open the top drawer, careful not to disturb the thick dust that lay evenly over the table and the variegated pink and white crocheted doily. The drawer was empty.

"I thought so," Elizabeth muttered.

"What are you looking for, Liz?" Avis asked and sat on the unmade bed. She thought Elizabeth was still under the influence of

Dr. Ryan's injection. Maybe food would uncloud her thinking. "I made brown-sugar brownies. Want one?"

"I want"—Elizabeth searched the large opening beneath the nightstand drawer—"the family Bible."

"Why?" Avis could not help asking, though she had no hope of getting a coherent answer.

"Because I noticed it was missing a few days ago." Elizabeth looked under the bed and reached around with her hands, pulling out nothing more than one and a half pairs of their father's favorite blue felt slippers. "The hole appeared in the living room bookcase where the Bible has always been just about the same day that our mother *dis*appeared. And *nothing* in this house ever moves unless *I* move it."

"Oh." Avis grunted and moved to rifle the dressing table between the two windows in the rear wall. "Probably doesn't mean anything," she said into an orphaned jewelry box crammed with costume pieces of forty years before. "I'll bet Jess just borrowed it to confirm a date or something for his research." But she didn't believe it.

Both daughters were unwilling to dig through their father's dresser unless absolutely necessary. Avis threw open the closet and stood back for an overview. The fact that she had no idea whatsoever where to look made the job tougher than she would have liked. Part of her prayed to spot a suspicious-looking shoe box or attaché case before she was reduced to going through Frank's pockets.

Elizabeth was on her hands and knees in front of the five-tier dresser. The dog-eared corner of a photograph, cardboard backing still attached, peeked out from beneath the bottom drawer. She pulled at it without much hope and felt more papers shinnying up behind the wood. Wriggling the corner slightly, she worked the photo into view.

It was a hand-tinted sixteen-by-twenty-inch studio portrait of a young girl, probably taken just before World War II. Elizabeth might have thought it was an antiqued picture of her own sister had she not known it was one of the last photos taken of their Aunt Arlene. She moved the photo aside on the floor and reached back underneath for the remaining items. When nothing was left, she spread the things for examination.

"What did you get?" Avis asked.

"Pictures," Elizabeth answered with disappointment. "I don't really know yet." There was a World War I military group shot she thought she recognized as having hung in the kitchen when her grandmother was alive; it had disappeared shortly after her death. Sal had always hated the shot and relegated it to the purgatory that was the barn. These were obviously the prints that had been in the old frames Frank had emptied and left in the gallery for reuse. There were several sepia-toned studio portraits of people she assumed were unidentified and forgotten ancestors. Avis abandoned her halfhearted search of the closet and sat on the floor next to Elizabeth.

"Don't mess up the order, Avis. I want to put these back so Dad doesn't know we were in here." *Unless we find something incriminating,* she thought. Every time she managed to get used to a frightening turn of events, another event turned.

Avis must have noticed the strong family resemblance between herself and her father's sister, because she was studying Aunt Arlene's portrait intently.

"Do I remember this?" she asked.

"I don't think so. Gramma Meg had it hanging in her room. You were pretty little when Gramma died and Mom cleaned everything out. Pretty, wasn't she?"

"How did she die, anyway? She was so young."

"Eight. I overheard Mom and Dad talking about it one day. They made me promise not to tell you, but I guess you're old enough now." Elizabeth sorted through three more photos before she continued. "It was yellowjackets. She stumbled into a ground hive during a picnic on Cap's Island. Dad was only four or five, but he remembered that Arlene looked like she was wearing a live suit of swarming insects. When she screamed, they filled her mouth. His mother picked Arlene up in her arms and ran to the shore. She threw the little girl into the ocean to drown the wasps off her body. Even after, dozens were stuck in her skin and had to be picked out, one at a time. By the time Gramma and Grampa got her back to the mainland, her heart had stopped."

"My God," Avis whispered, thinking that no one was ever really old enough to hear a story like that one. "No wonder Dad would never take us to Cap's." She ran her hand over the face frozen at eight years old and imagined what it must be like to lose a child. Impossible and too terrible. Suddenly she was aware of the thickness of the image she held in her hands. The tape that secured the photo to the backing was yellow and cracked. As she put it back on the pile, the backing slid away from the picture. "Damn." she reached for it to see what damage she had done and a brittle parchment fell heavily to the carpet, snapping off a previously cracked corner. "Damn!"

"What?"

"Oh, just damn," Avis grumbled nervously and picked crumbled paper out of the carpet. "The backing on this picture just disintegrated on me."

"Let me see that," Elizabeth ordered. The parchment was as crumbly as phyllo pastry and fell into four clean segments where it had been folded. "Well," Elizabeth commented to herself, "I was wondering how I was going to get it open without damaging it. Looks like I couldn't." Carefully she turned each piece writing side up and laid them out in order on the floor.

As with all old handmade paper, the exterior edges of the document were wavy. The parchment had aged to a pale ivory, the ink washed to a dull but still legible mud color. Several flakes of crisp red material were brushed into the rug. Elizabeth recognized it as wax fallen from the lower portion of the page; a vaguely circular smudge marked its original position. Avis hovered over her sister's shoulder.

"It's old, isn't it? I mean *really* old."

"I'd say," Elizabeth agreed. "See the script? That word 'witneff' is supposed to be 'witness.' I can't remember when Americans stopped using that style of penmanship. It's really lovely, though. I wish the ink had held up better. There are places that are so faded, they're kind of hard to make out. Grab Dad's reading glasses off the nightstand, would you?"

Avis quickly stood and retrieved the glasses. Handing them to Elizabeth, she asked, "What is it?"

"My God," Elizabeth breathed. She slid the spectacles over her nose and leaned closer to the page.

"What? How old is it, anyway?"

"April, 1765." Elizabeth pushed her sister out of the light.

"So? This house is almost a hundred years older than that. What is it?"

Elizabeth leaned back, rump on heels, and handed the glasses to Avis.

"It's a King's Charter awarded to one Captain Josiah Will. It deeds him full ownership to an entire island 'hence to be called Will's Isle' in recognition of his loyalty and productivity to the Crown."

"Cool." Avis bent over the document. "Does this mean we're heiresses?" She put on and removed her father's glasses several times. "I never heard of a Will's Isle."

"There isn't one." Elizabeth pointed to a paragraph buried in the calligraphic mass at the center of the document. "This gives the location as south and east down the water break from Smith's Isle forever deeded to the Will family on the one condition that Josiah's descendants inhabit the island continuously for the following hundred years. That would have been until 1865. Unlikely he accomplished that, I'd say, since this house has been in the family since way before then."

"What difference does a contingency make if the island doesn't exist?" Avis returned the glasses to the nightstand.

"Oh, it exists. But I'm betting the name got shortened over the years. The island located south and east of Smith's Isle is now called Cap's Island, after Captain Josiah, no doubt."

"I'll be damned." Avis smiled. "We're landed gentry."

"Oh, wake up, Avis," Elizabeth chided, "we'd know something like that. This charter has been nothing more than backing material since"—she glanced at the photo of Arlene Will—"at least since this picture was framed. Over fifty years, at least." She replaced the charter behind the photo and covered it with the cardboard stiffener. Then she meticulously piled the pictures in their original order to slide back under Frank's bureau. But before she did, she snuck a look at the back of each print, looking for a similar discolored outline. Where had the charter been kept before being slid into the frame with Aunt Arlene? "Besides," she said, ending the discussion, "as far as I know, all the King's grants were repealed during the War of 1812. Remember?"

"I guess I do, now that you mention it. Isn't that why the Portsmouth Shipyard is really in Kittery now?"

"Right." But was it? That was a problem with historic areas: too much history and too many dates. Obviously Cap's Island had changed hands at some point, or Elizabeth and Frank would be fishing out of Cap's instead of Sagamore Creek. Elizabeth reminded herself not to assume anything.

She assumed her father was innocent, but that was only out of loyalty. She had never been able to take anything for granted regarding him. And who could she assume had folded the old parchment and stashed it behind a photograph that called up such horrific memories? It could have been her grandmother, but it was her father who—out of the blue—had emptied all the frames and secreted the contents under a bureau in his room.

She assumed (forgetting entirely that she'd decided to assume nothing) there was no good reason for any of it. If the Will family still owned Cap's Island, Frank would not oppose legalized gambling. Another assumption: Sale of the island would keep the Will family in dog food and lobster stew for the rest of their lives. On the other hand, if Frank did have a claim to the property, Al Jenness the realtor would have been a good friend to have. It could be Frank's best defense against what was shaping up as a solid murder charge. Elizabeth had lost count of her assumptions.

There were only two ways to find out who owned Cap's Island. The hard way, through weeks or months of research for which she did not have the time—or the easy way, by figuring out how to ask Jesse about the chronology of territorial possession he had already established without raising his suspicions. She knew she could not trust her own foggy memories from stiflingly dull classes in local history at Dovekey Beach Junior High. She would have to find the Bible.

Another twenty minutes revealed nothing more out of the ordinary in Frank and Sal's room.

The sisters put everything as neatly back in place as they could, doused the light, and returned to the living room, where Elizabeth immediately tuned in to her favorite movie of all time, *The Haunting,* starring Julie Harris. Avis watched quietly for several minutes until her nerves started to get the better of her.

"Liz?" she asked. Julie Harris was walking down a long hallway looking both terrified and entranced. "Why are we looking for the family Bible? Liz?"

Avis covered Elizabeth with the afghan and let her sleep. Though she did not move a limb, Elizabeth's dreams were a maelstrom of swirling and stinging bees, falling seagulls, and tumbling ruins of crushed numerals.

SIXTEEN

GINNY SAT AT Ben Ryan's kitchen table alternately sipping coffee and rubbing her temples.

"You ought to take something for that," the doctor advised.

"Take two aspirin and call you in the morning?"

"Don't believe in aspirin. Hard on the stomach." Ryan refilled their coffee cups and joined her at the table. Edith was at her weekly chair-caning lesson. "Thanks for transcribing those notes for me."

"Thank *you*. Wish I knew any more than I did before." It was just nine o'clock in the morning and Ginny could hear the rustlings of patients patiently waiting for their appointments in Ryan's attached office. "The second pathologist's opinion didn't shed any additional light on the subject, either. I'm just plain stumped."

"What's the question?"

"I beg your pardon?" Ginny asked.

"In medical school, we were taught to ask ourselves what's the question." Ryan lit a cigarette. "If you answer *the* question, all the *other* questions you believe you have will be answered. What is your bottom-line question?"

"Right now, who shoved Al Jenness into that lobster trap and sunk him."

"Good." The doctor threw a piece of toast to the dog under the table. "Good. Once we know who tried to hide the crime, we'll have a better chance of finding out who did the crime and why. Right?"

"Right." It seemed so simple put that way. No names, no friends, no murder. Just who tied the knot. "The lab returned the trap head to you, didn't they?"

"Sure. It's right here in the breezeway. Edith covered it with an old towel. Said looking at it was ruining her appetite." Ginny could relate to that. "The laboratory only needed a quarter inch off the end of the mending twine to compare with the samples you gave me. I dropped them off last night after I left Frank and Elizabeth's."

"Great." Ginny lifted the towel. It looked just as she remembered it. Her headache returned in a great gush of pain. "I don't know what I'm looking for, Doctor. It looks like fishing equipment to me."

"*The* question, Ginny."

"Who tied the knot." She picked up the netting and rolled it over her fingers. "It's a damned knot. Just a damned knot, and a bass-ackwards one at that. This isn't helping me."

Ryan took the head from Ginny. "What do you mean, bass-ackwards?"

She walked back into the kitchen for more coffee. Ryan replaced the evidence under the towel and followed her.

"It's a plain old square knot, except backwards."

"I don't understand," the doctor prodded in his best bedside manner.

"Weren't you ever a Girl Scout? A square knot is right over left and under, left over right and under. Standing over the body, the ends of the knot would be on the bottom left and top right. The knot is backwards. Vice versa."

"Less efficient?"

134

"Not at all. Just backwards."

"So, we know the person who threw Al Jenness over the side doesn't know how to make a proper square knot. What else do we know?"

"Of course!" Ginny smiled genuinely for the first time in days. "Strength. It would take a lot of muscle to wrestle the body into position, and even more to toss it over the side of the boat." Her smile faded abruptly. "Terrific. We're looking for a faceless male—with a boat—who was never a Boy Scout."

"Don't assume, Ginny. I know several women strong enough to pitch a body into the water." He looked over the lip of his mug. "So do you."

Elizabeth was stronger than most men.

So much for the benefits of clean living and the work ethic, thought Ginny.

Elizabeth woke up sweating on the sofa, her legs cruelly pinned to the sagging cushions.

"Get off!" she kicked. *"Off!"*

Petunia grudgingly rolled to the floor and wandered to the kitchen. Avis was staring morosely into a bowl of Rice Krispies; Elizabeth could hear the feeble snap, crackle, and pop.

"Dad didn't come home last night," Avis said and put the bowl on the floor for the dog to finish.

"Are you sure?" Elizabeth asked.

"Am I *sure?* After two horror movies in a row, do you seriously believe I closed my eyes all night? I guess he just left from Jesse's this morning. Probably wanted to let you sleep it off."

"Bull," Elizabeth responded. "What time is it?"

"A little past nine."

Elizabeth looked down to remind herself what outfit she had fallen asleep in the night before, looked out the window at a sunny day, and deemed herself well enough dressed to head directly out.

"You try to get ahold of Mom this morning?"

Avis nodded. "No answer. Called her boyfriend, too. He doesn't know where she is."

Elizabeth stopped in her tracks. "Bob the Ubiquitous doesn't know where she is?" Their mother's newest beau was a full fifteen years younger than she and stuck by her side like Velcro. For the first time, Avis and Elizabeth took Sal's inaccessibility seriously. "C'mon, Avis, let's make sure we haven't misplaced our father, too."

Ben Ryan stared into the trunk of the police cruiser. The bright sunlight exposed the grotesque bodies, lying on their beds of plastic.

"Sandy seems to have summed it all up," Ryan assessed, prodding both seagulls with a tongue depressor he had brought outside. "Except one thing." He pointed to the dried-up carcass of the bird that had been shot. "See the striations on the neck?" He pushed aside a choker of broken feathers. "This one was hung, too."

Frank's bull moose of a truck stood vigil over the salt-water creek. The dock was deserted; it was too early for pleasure cruisers, too late for commercial boaters, except for an oily young man with overlong hair who'd been left to tend the gas pump. His sneakered feet hung over the rail; a hand line waiting to be pounced upon by an errant flounder dangled from his hand. The *Curmudgeon II* rolled passively at her mooring. Jesse's dory was tied to his marker buoy twenty feet away from the empty *Curmudgeon*.

"Hey, Efram!" Elizabeth called to the boy. He gave his hand line a tentative tug to see if he'd hooked anything and then laid the spool aside.

"Yeah?"

"You see my dad here this morning?"

"Frank?"

"Yeah. You see him?"

"Was he here this mornin'?"

Exasperated, Elizabeth untied the Will dory from the dock. She tossed the rope to Avis. "That's what I'm asking you, Efram."

"Oh, Liz," he answered slowly, picking up the spool once more. "I don't know. S'been wicked busy this mornin'."

Elizabeth gestured for her sister to get into the small rowboat. "I can see that, Efram."

"What?"

"Bye, Efram. If my dad comes by, let him know I took the boat out, okay?"

"What?"

The town clerk's office was located conveniently in Asa and Maggie Fleck's living room on Benning Way, just off the beach road. Maggie had a blue plastic-covered card table and painted-to-match file cabinet she'd picked up at a yard sale set aside expressly for town business in one corner, next to the new Wurlitzer organ. There were plastic bins from K Mart, color-coded according to Maggie's own system: brown for dog licenses, red for fire violations, green for zoning ordinances, purple for criminal stuff, putty for building permits, black for divorces, and bridal white for marriage licenses. If she did say so herself, it was one hell of a system, especially on an annual salary of $7,300.

Ginny knocked twice on the Justice of the Peace sign on the front door and walked in. Maggie was in her bathrobe, talking on her chicken-fat yellow wall phone. She held up her finger to let Ginny know she'd be right with her, and whispered, "Gotta go, Claire. Police business." She hung up, torn as to whether it was worth giving Ginny attitude in retaliation for her being so snotty the day they brought in Al Jenness's body, at the cost of missing out on some official inside information. *Pride goeth before a fall,* she solemnly preached to herself and said with admirable professional composure, "What can I do for you, Chief?"

"I'd like to look up some records, Maggie." Ginny eyed the plastic bins with less appreciation than awe and added, "Might need your help."

Maggie Fleck was more gratified than she had hoped. She quickly hooked the neck of her patterned chenille robe and re-cinched the belt to get down to business. She would have first dibs on whatever Ginny was looking for.

"What can I get for you, Chief?"

Ginny kept her face impassive. The title "Chief" always made her feel as though she were running *The Daily Planet* and not a police department.

"Title documents and a decree of divorce. I don't have firm dates for any of them, is that going to be a problem?"

"Would be in New York." Maggie could not stop herself from drawing out the name of the city, but went on quickly. "But divorces are cross-indexed here by name. It's a small town. Property titles might be tougher, but give me the names of the residents and the locations of the land and I'll see what I can do."

It rankled Ginny to be giving Maggie so much pleasure, but there was no way around it short of digging through the county records.

"The title search is for Cap's Island, maybe under the name Garrett Selby, maybe the organization the Children of Deity."

Maggie's round face fell. "Oh, title searches are done every time there's a transfer of property and are given to the bank to guarantee the transfer is legal. Sometimes the realtor or buyer will keep a copy, but usually not since it'll just have to be redone on the next sale. A law passed by lawyers, no doubt. Costs a *fortune*. Any-way"—Maggie took a breath—"all I have here are executed deeds and town surveys."

Disappointed, Ginny realized it would not be as easy as she

had hoped. "Okay," she answered, "I'd like what you have for the island, then, for as far back as you can go."

"Sorry. Records for the islands aren't kept here. The territory has changed jurisdictions so many times, all records are kept on the islands themselves."

"When did that happen?"

"Oh, let me think, since 'seventy or so."

"Well, that's not so bad. You were town clerk then, start me out with what you remember."

Maggie took on an affronted posture. "Eighteen-seventy or so." She remembered her mission, to learn what she could about the investigation. "But the Athenaeum might have copies, if you don't want to go back out to Cap's."

"Might isn't good enough, Maggie. Where are the records located at the islands?"

"Always stored in the churches. I know that's not a very good separation of church and state, but there you have it. There's only one church left out there these days, and that would be the one on Cap's run by those weirdos. You gonna need a court order or anything?"

Ginny shook her head, hoping it would not be necessary. If it had been full summer she could have sent Mr. Elwell to Exeter to petition the judge, but it was not, and Ginny was as busy as a one-armed paper hanger.

"How about the divorce decree?"

"Well, as long as it was granted after 1922, I'll have it here. Course there weren't many divorces happening before then, were there? What's the name?"

"Will. Frank and Sally Will." Ginny wanted a cigarette. Desperately. A cigarette and a cherry Coke, and she wanted to be a little girl again playing in Frank and Sal's backyard because they never cared if the grass got dug up. She did not notice the significant pause.

"Don't have one," Maggie said, surprised. She had always thought the police knew almost as much as she did about the private lives of her neighbors. "Sal and Frank never filed for divorce."

"What?"

"Strange, I know, what with her taking off for Boston, oh, what, ten or eleven years ago. I'd guess she had enough of squaring off with Frank after all those years and just decided it wasn't worth it to fight to the finish. The only reason she'd need a divorce would be if she wanted to get married again, and after being married to Frank, I figure she'd have lost her taste for that. Besides, the way it is, she gets everything if anything happens to Frank."

"Excuse me?"

"Well, you didn't ask about last wills and testaments. I don't have those on record until there's actually a deceased, of course—that's probated there in the gray bin—but I take ceramics with Frank's lawyer's secretary and she told me—"

"Frank never changed his will after Sal left."

"Right. And it was a real complicated one, she told me. All kinds of codicils and such forbidding the girls from inheriting this and that." Maggie leaned close conspiratorially. "Quite a screaming match over that one between Frank and Sal, I don't mind telling you."

Avis appropriated wads of Frank's discarded clothing to wear from the hooks under the canopy in case the weather was cold outside the harbor, but the late-morning sun was firing efficiently and both women were comfortable in what they had worn from the house. Elizabeth pulled three traps on the way out to confirm that Frank had not worked the line that morning. Dried salt speckled and streaked the front of her clothing where she had splashed water off the pots. Piscatawk and Cap's islands guarded the horizon, flat and unbroken except for a local cruise ship on its scheduled tour of the Isle of Shoals three miles farther out.

"Jesse's not here, Liz. Why don't you try the radio again?"

"We've tried every frequency I can think of. He's not answering. Besides, we don't *know* he's not here." Elizabeth gunned the engine and pulled the wheel hard to the right. "He might be at the north side. He keeps some traps off the ledge for spider crabs."

"Wouldn't it be faster to go between the islands instead of around the big one?" Avis asked, feeling a bit seasick. "Do you have any Dramamine?"

"First-aid kit, bolted right there." Elizabeth pointed to the left of the door into the hold. "Wash it down with some Dr Pepper. Sugar will help." She watched Avis medicate herself and then continued, "Can't go between. Water's too shallow."

"Oh." Avis grunted weakly. "I think I'm going to throw up, Biz."

"No, you're not. Watch the horizon, that'll settle you right down. Besides, we're almost round. If we don't spot the *Celia T.* I'll let you drive the way home. That'll do you." But Avis got a reprieve when the women spotted Jesse's boat floating five hundred yards north beyond the center of Cap's Island. A scuba flag flew from the antenna, and a red buoy with white stripes bobbed just off the *Celia T.*'s aft.

"What the hell," Elizabeth muttered to herself and throttled down to come aside. Jesse would not dive alone, so that pretty much settled it that Frank had tagged along. As expected, the boat was empty.

"I can't believe they're diving today," said Avis and chugged her soda.

Elizabeth raised binoculars to her eyes and scanned the surface of the water. Church bells tolled loudly from Cap's, immediately met with amplified rock music from Piscatawk. It was a decibel war. Hearing the bells up close, she could sympathize with Cap's neighbors. It was enough to wake the dead. Finally, when the din subsided, she said, "I don't think they *are* diving." She handed the binoculars to her sister. "You see a safety line to the boat or any bubbles coming to the surface?"

Avis looked hard before answering, "No." She double-checked the water. "You don't think something happened to them, do you? You don't think, uh . . ."

"They're dead?" Elizabeth eased the *Curmudgeon* away and headed back around Piscatawk. "I think we'd better check out Cap's Island."

"Couldn't you go in after them and see if they *are* down?"

"Could, if I'd brought the equipment, but I didn't. If I go in without a wet suit, hypothermia will get me in less than three minutes."

"Shouldn't we call Ginny?"

"Sure, go ahead, but by the time she gets out here, we'll know what's going on anyway. If Dad and Jesse are dead, they'll still be dead later."

The Siren's call of the cherry Coke was too compelling for Ginny to ignore, and Foye's Pharmacy was only five hundred yards from the police station, so she walked over and submitted. Jake Foye himself prepared the soda with extra syrup, just the way Ginny liked it. The Drake sisters came in on their monthly Medicare jaunt shortly after Ginny was served, so she was left to her own thoughts while Mr. Foye filled the elderly twins' prescriptions.

She pondered *the* question, but to get to the bottom line, she had to travel from the top. What was Al Jenness doing out at sea the night he died? Ginny didn't even know whether Al owned a boat, but she could find that out easily enough. Probably it didn't matter. However Al made it to the spot where he was discovered, someone else had to have gotten the transportation away. Whoever owned the boat was most likely the person who sank Al.

Ginny still found it hard to believe that no one on Cap's Island had noticed anything the night of the murder, but Garrett

Selby had been adamant. No one had seen anything. If it had been tourist season, a witness might have been found in Dovekey Beach to testify to a late-night excursion—but it was not, and no resident had seen a boat pull out that evening after the Town Meeting.

Frank found the body. The body was in Frank's trap. There were rumors that Al was sleeping with Frank's daughter. Will's Cottage on Cap's Island would surely be taken for Al's legislated gambling. Now Frank's wife—not ex-wife, but wife—was missing.

It still did not float for Ginny. She tossed two dollars on the soda-fountain counter and started back to the station. While unfairly cursing the murder victim, she noticed a van parked next to Ruth Jenness's Town Car in the driveway of the realty office. There was a luminescent cross spray-painted on the side panel—not the sympathy-call style of Reverend Rogler from the Dovekey Congregationalist Church. Besides, the church was directly across the road; Reverend Rogler would not drive ten feet to give Ruth his condolences. Ginny sensed she was about to be saved another long, wet trip out to the islands.

When the door chime announced Ginny's entrance, Ruth Jenness and Garrett Selby looked up from where they were seated at Al Jenness's desk. Books and papers spilled from Selby's lap. He hurriedly organized the fallen documents and placed them in a large leather briefcase.

"Sorry to startle you two," Ginny said. She walked to the back of the room, chose a mug, and poured herself a cup of coffee from the machine on the filing cabinet behind Ruth.

The Widow Jenness stood. "Oh, I thought I had the Closed sign on the door."

"You did," Ginny said, "but the door wasn't locked and I saw you had company, so I just barged on in." She sipped thoughtfully. "Sorry." Brazenly she leaned in front of Ruth and looked at the papers on the desk. The desk calendar was still open to the first half of the week. The real estate business apparently stank. The only entry for the day before Al died was the beginning of a grocery list: Cod.

Ruth sat down and nervously stacked and straightened. She handed Selby an oversized leatherbound book, which he slid into his briefcase. "May I?" Ginny asked with her hand outstretched toward the book.

Selby snapped the case shut and smiled at Ginny. "I didn't realize you were interested in spiritual matters, Chief Philbrick. I have to get back to the island now, but I would be pleased to set up a counseling appointment with you." He smiled again.

"Is that what I interrupted?"

"Yes," Ruth answered. "Yes. I asked the Reverend Selby to counsel me during my bereavement." Ginny lifted what looked like a blueprint from in front of Ruth and idly perused it. It was an architectural survey of Cap's Island. *Bingo!* Something Maggie had in her bureaucratic bins.

Ruth carefully pulled the survey from Ginny's hand. "As a matter of fact, I'm going to be joining the Reverend on his island retreat." She gave the paper to Selby, who folded it and slipped it into a jacket pocket. "This has been more difficult than you could imagine, Ginny."

"Well, well," Selby cut in, "I have to be going if I'm to make afternoon services. Mrs. Jenness, I'll be calling again. Good to see you, Chief; I hope the investigation is going well. Perhaps you will visit us again sometime."

Ginny shook his hand. "You can count on it."

"Yes, well, that's good. Yes, well, good-bye then."

"Oh, Reverend." Ginny stopped him. "It seems there's been a Peeping Tom reported on Piscatawk. We can't figure out how he gets on the island, so for the sake of your female guests, you might want to beef up your security."

"A voyeur out at the islands?" Selby seemed genuinely

shocked. "Well, thank you for the warning, Chief. Thank you. I'll keep an eye out." The minister shuttled away, a frown creasing his forehead. He could not think of one woman in his parish who would tempt any man, no matter how decadent, to sail seven miles out to sea for a surreptitious peek.

Ruth turned her back on the door before Selby was out and forced a manila envelope into the filing cabinet behind the desk.

Ginny pushed her advantage. "I couldn't help but notice the architectural survey you two were going over. Did Selby give you the contract to sell Will's Cottage, Ruth?"

Ruth stiffened but did not hesitate on her way back to her own desk, where she sat and waited for Ginny. "Will's Cottage? Oh, you mean the caretaker's cottage at the retreat." She tucked an escaped strand of hair back into her coiffure. "Heavens, no. That's a part of the complex. Reverend Selby offered me the use of the house while I stay out there, that's all." When Ginny did not react, Ruth continued, "This has been a terrible time for me, Ginny. There are a lot of things you don't know."

Ginny sat in the chair next to the desk. "Tell me."

"Al was having an affair." Ruth drew in a long breath and reached into the top drawer in front of her. She handed a blue-backed legal document to Ginny. "Al was planning to divorce me so he could marry the other woman."

Ginny sped through the legalese in her hand. Sure enough, Al Jenness had taken great trouble to pave the way to divorce. But no corespondent was named. There was no documentation of the identity of the woman with whom Al had been having his affair—or even that there *was* an affair. Still, wives tend to know these things. "Who?" Ginny asked.

"Elizabeth Will."

Ginny swallowed hard at the confirmation of her own suspicions. "How do you know?"

"Love letters. Dozens of them in a lockbox Al kept hidden at home. If he hadn't been killed, I never would have found them."

"This is a motive for Al's murder, you know."

"I know. When Frank Will threatened my husband, I thought it was political. Now, of course, I know it was because of his daughter."

"Frank threatened Al?"

"Several times. Now I wish I had reported it. When I found the letters, I thought to tell you about it, but the evidence seemed so conclusive, I didn't see any reason to drag us all through the mud."

"May I see the letters, Ruth?"

Ruth cleared her throat. "I burned them. I burned everything. You understand."

Elizabeth and Avis tied the *Curmudgeon* to the Cap's Island wharf and raced up the steep path to the hotel. Avis slipped and almost fell several times on the rocky path. The two women were not stopped at the door to the enclave, nor were their knocks answered from within. The sound of hymn-singing washed into the main building from the church behind it. The bells had been a call to worship.

"Let's find a phone. There must be one here. That way we can be sure to get a message to Ginny onshore through somebody." Elizabeth noted the profound absence of clutter in the unoccupied rooms on her right and left. "After we call, we'll search the grounds." The huge industrial kitchen was immaculate, deserted, and phoneless as well. Elizabeth pledged to herself that should she find Frank alive and well, she would kill him. The last door in the long hall was ajar, and through the six-inch crack Avis spotted a telephone on the left side of a large walnut desk. Without hesitating, she swung open the door and went directly to call the police.

Neither Avis nor her sister saw the man behind the door, bent over the powdery journals.

Avis nearly wept at the sound of a dial tone in her ear. Elizabeth had passed the desk and was staring out the window toward the cottage. The bow of the abandoned *Celia T.* was barely visible on the right. "What's the number, Liz?" Avis asked.

"Up," answered Eli Selby, stepping from behind the paneled door, a revolver pointed in the women's direction. "Your number is up." The sisters froze. The telephone dropped from Avis's hand at her ear.

Eli relaxed. If these were the intruders his brother was so worried about, then things were not so bad after all. It had been too long since Eli had shared a room with an attractive woman. It had been *much* too long since he had shared a room with two.

"I'm sorry," Avis apologized automatically and replaced the receiver.

"We're looking for our father. He's missing. We thought we'd call the police from here and then search the island," Elizabeth explained.

"Well, well," Eli said, taking on the speech pattern he had unconsciously acquired from his brother, "no one is allowed on this island unless they are an invited guest." He pulled a flask from his pocket, took a sip, and offered it to Elizabeth, still holding the gun steady at his waist. She stole a quick glance out the window. Jesse's boat was gone. Smiling encouragingly, she inched to her left to make certain the *Celia T.* had pulled out. It had.

"Thank you." Elizabeth edged toward Eli and accepted the flask. "I'm sorry we broke in like this, but my sister tends to overreact." She smiled again and turned to Avis, shooting her a "keep your mouth shut, I'll handle this" look. She swallowed a mouthful of whiskey and thrust out her hand. "My name is Elizabeth, and this is my sister, Avis. I'm really sorry."

Eli paused only a moment before laying aside his pistol to shake the strawberry blond's hand and nod to the brunette. Then, to show his good intentions, he put the gun out of sight, behind his back in the waistband of his slacks. Neither Elizabeth nor Avis was particularly reassured.

"S'okay. I got a brother who flies off the handle, too. As a matter of fact, he's due back any time now and it'd be a good idea if you were gone." Elizabeth was looking at the disarray at his feet; papers and books were strewn everywhere. "He'll shit a brick if I don't clean this up, too, so you better get going." Elizabeth was no more than two feet from Eli and looked directly up into his eyes. Hers were that green that made him so crazy. God, he missed women. "I'll walk you both down to the dock, so you don't get lost or anything."

"That's kind of you. We appreciate it, don't we, Avis?" Avis did not answer, so Elizabeth made the first move toward the door. She watched her feet, careful not to kick the papers on the polished floor: originals and a pile of copies still warm from the desktop copier winking its red eye nearby. Still, somehow, she slid on a slick sheet and ended up on her rear end. She looked so adorably sheepish that Eli, not generally the most chivalrous of God's creatures, helped the obviously mortified woman to her feet. "C'mon, Avis," Elizabeth urged, thanking Eli with her eyes. "Dad's probably waiting for us at home."

Eli accompanied the women to their boat, relieved that his brother's craft was not in sight. He watched Elizabeth's buttocks with fascination as she boarded the *Curmudgeon*. He cast off, throwing the rope to Avis.

"Hey," he called to Elizabeth, who had taken her position behind the wheel. "Maybe I could call you sometime, you know?"

She threw the engine into reverse and continued to show him her most pleasant face. "Sure. That would be nice."

Eli grinned and waved. He could not get off the island, but here was a terrific-looking babe who could get herself on.

"Hey, wait. I don't have your number."

The boat was pulling slowly away, Avis looking sick again.

"I'm in the book," Elizabeth answered, concentrating on getting as far from Cap's Island and the man with the gun as she could.

"What's your last name?"

"Will," she called back without thinking. She would bite her tongue later, when she had the luxury.

"What?" Eli screamed back.

Relieved she hadn't been heard, Elizabeth just waved goodbye and threw the throttle to full.

"Are you *nuts?*" Avis shrieked when it was safe. "There's a man with a gun on that island, and we still haven't found Dad. That guy might have shot him and Jesse, too."

"Jesse's boat is gone. Wherever the two of them were on or under the island, they left." Elizabeth plucked a beer from the cooler on deck. It was warm, but she didn't care. "Take the wheel, Avis, before you upchuck." She twisted the cap off by jamming the top into the inside of her forearm and then, holding the cap tight against her skin with her right hand, rotated her left arm away from her body. The cap fell into the slatwork at her feet. It was one of her favorite "manly man" tricks. "And looky, looky what we have here," she announced, pulling papers from the rear waistband of her pants. (Her *new* favorite "manly man" trick.)

"Did you steal those?" Avis asked in horror.

"Sure did." Elizabeth gulped half the beer from the bottle and studied the copies. "Know what I have here?" She did not wait for an answer. "I have a copy of a handwritten copy of the charter we found in Dad's room last night. And"—she waved the paper in her sister's face—"stapled to it is a copy of more—and I'll just bet you, explanatory—copies of other stuff."

Avis turned away from the wheel. "You grabbed those when you pretended to fall." She shook her head as though to clear it. "You could have gotten us shot to death over *paper.*" Elizabeth finished her beer. Avis went back to her driving. "If you weren't so stupid, I'd think you were really cool."

Elizabeth took another beer out of the Styrofoam. "Try not to suck a trap line into the rotor while I read, okay?"

SEVENTEEN

GINNY AND SANDY'S apartment in the Parsonage carriage house spread light from its tiny windows into the surrounding pine trees, over the rhododendrons planted by the side entrance, and up the long drive toward the main road. A nearly full moon on the wane tossed a light blanket of green over the shadows.

The living room, simple and neat during the day, took on a garish and deserted air in the artificial light. The steamer trunk that did double duty as a coffee table was covered in research texts, notes Ginny had made to herself, and the framed 1880-something portrait of Lydia Will she had set up facing the leather sofa, in hopes the weathered face and sad eyes would somehow tell her a story she needed to know. Ginny picked the picture up and spoke softly, so as not to wake Sandy in the next room.

"What do you know, old lady? Were you watching the night Al Jenness died, or are you weeding your garden somewhere in Paradise?" Ginny held the frame aloft to better judge how her friend Elizabeth resembled her great-whatever grandmother. The set of the mouth, perhaps. The arch of the brows, for sure. Ginny had always been sorry her family had gotten rid of so many old things, but her parents had been assiduously modern in their thinking and tossed photos whenever it was determined that no one remembered who they pictured anymore. She had begged her own mother to write identities down on the reverse of the pictures, but it had never happened. Ginny flipped to the back of the carved walnut frame. The brads that secured the thin wooden backing were mostly gone. Those that remained were loose or bent. Staring out the window at the eerie moonglow, Ginny fiddled with the tiny nails. One by one they dropped and she found herself idly lifting the thin cracked wood out of the frame. With a smile of admiration, she read the handwritten note on the back of the portrait.

It read, "Lydia Haley Will in her garden. Captain's Island, July 4, 1880." The penmanship was shaky but legible, probably Lydia's own hand. Ginny tried to remember the Cap's Island she had visited, comparing it in her mind with the picture in her hand. The building being erected behind Lydia must be the Children of Deity house. Lydia must have been facing toward Will's Cottage. Perhaps the photographer had been standing in her doorway.

Ginny replaced the backing and reminded herself to advise Elizabeth to do something to preserve the old portrait. A large discoloration had already appeared on the back. It would be a shame if the damage spread to the entire piece.

Suddenly Ginny dug her nails back into the frame, lifting the wood once more and setting it aside. The discoloration had not come from water or sun damage. It was a regular outline, darkened only on the back and at its perimeter, as though something had been stored between the photo and the wood for many years. Small, about seven inches by ten inches, not the size of another photograph. Instinctively she collected the brads and examined the holes they had left in the dry wood. When she turned it for examination, the backing cracked down its center.

"Damn," she cursed aloud.

"You all right, Gin?" Sandy called sleepily from the next room.

"Fine, Sandy. I'm fine. Go back to sleep."

The slightly oily dust that coated the brads, along with the clean indentations they had left, convinced Ginny that whatever had been hidden behind Lydia Haley Will had been removed many years before.

Terrific, she groused to herself. *Just what I need: a mystery from the last century, when I can't solve the one I've already got.* In disgust she turned out the light, leaving the mess on the steamer trunk to be cleaned up in the morning.

"What's one more mess?" she asked herself, and went to bed.

Charles MacKay sat bolt upright in bed, his heart jackhammering in his chest, his ears filled with the stab of a Valkyrie scream. One second he was at rest, the next he was on his feet, thrusting his legs into a pair of jeans that had been lying in a muddle next to his bed. He ran barefoot at top speed down the antiseptic white-tiled hall, propelling himself around a dim corner and into the maintenance office. In the darkness, he ricocheted off the gray metal desk and reached desperately for the wall. Slamming his fists against it over and over, he finally crippled the panel that controlled the sensor alarm. The school-style clock behind the desk read 2:00.

The tidal wave of silence was a welcome suffocation.

MacKay's island had once more been breached, but this time the culprit had triggered the security system. It was strange that the scientist had not planned or given instruction in how to shut down the sirens placed strategically around the complex. The sounding of the system was the order for all personnel to report to the cafeteria building to be assigned a search area by the chief of security—an effeminate assistant professor of hydrology whom MacKay had privately dubbed "the water boy." Before

MacKay reached the path to the meeting hall, his arm was grasped from behind.

Debra, the long-suffering victim of the Piscatawk peeper, had refused to leave the island until she had completed her course of study. MacKay had respected her decision. She had, however, left the room in which she had listened for hours to the death throes of a tortured seagull—for the questionable comfort and bed of the water boy. MacKay did not respect that decision at all.

"He may still be in my room," Debra shouted above the confused chatter and slapping of feet on tile. Her perfect legs carried her away and back toward the west wing while the sleep-numbed MacKay processed her statement. In twenty long strides he caught up with his assistant.

At the door to her vacant room, Debra looked annoyed at MacKay's sign-language order to remain off to the side. MacKay was annoyed that he was not in possession of a weapon. Wearing only blue jeans as he was, his options were limited, to say the least. Feeling moronically unprepared, he lifted a fire extinguisher from its clamp on the wall, swung it over his back with his right hand, and sprung the door handle with his left.

Light from the overhead fixture slapped MacKay, who *had* thought to be ready for darkness. Debra pushed past him into the bedroom.

The venetian blinds dangled askew at the open window; wet sand and pebbles smeared the beige linoleum; reference books lay torn apart and splayed on broken backs; bedclothes had been ripped from the glorified cot and rearranged into what most closely resembled the maniacally constructed nest of an oversized bird. Within the nest lay neither egg nor hatchling.

Nestled in its makeshift cradle lay a twelve-by-twenty-four-inch grave marker. It was brutally chipped and sodden with slick algae. Despite the missing chinks and slimy vegetation, the lettering read shallow but clear in the bright light.

REST IN PEACE
SWEET DAUGHTER OF THE SEA
ELIZABETH WILL

Flickering candles reflected off Avis's fixed and dilated pupils. Her eyes seemed shrunken and hollow in the dancing glow where she lay on the floor beside the inert body of her sister.

One of Elizabeth's arms had fallen away from her body, the palm facing upward as though in supplication. The dog that should have been their protection was nowhere to be seen. Their father had, mercifully for him, not returned to the scene. A mouth opened in a soundless scream.

The mantel clock chimed three o'clock.

Click. Amy Irving shrieked and woke from her endless nightmare. The credits of Elizabeth's viewing choice of the evening, *Carrie,* rolled.

"Liz?" Avis was frightened into a whisper. "Liz?"

"Hghrgg."

"Elizabeth Will," Avis commanded, "you wake up *now.*" Elizabeth's eyelashes fluttered heavily. "How the *hell* can you sleep through this shit?" Avis hit the remote control rapidly, over and over, coming up with scratchy static on most of the channels.

"Is it over?" Elizabeth muttered. She opened one eye. "Did Dad get home?"

"No. It's past three and he's still missing."

Frank's daughters were now merely aggravated, since Efram the dock hand had told them, when they moored the *Curmudgeon,* that they had just missed Frank and Jesse. Of course they both had seen Jesse's *Celia T.* tied up as soon as they hit the mouth of the creek, but it was reassuring to *know* that Frank was with him and not floating face down in the Atlantic. Or retired in South American obscurity living off his mysterious ill-gotten gains. On the plus side, his absence meant that they could study the hijacked documents from Garrett Selby's library in a leisurely way.

Elizabeth had correctly recognized the top paper as a hand-rendered copy of the royal grant of lands to Josiah Will in 1765. The copy had not been made recently, judging by the style of the writing and the quality of the paper, but it was painstaking. No Xerox technology, she guessed, when the duplicate had been required.

The sheet directly below the first was an 1812 federal declaration made by the United States of America rescinding all land grants made by any other government before Independence. Any dreams of ownership of anything besides the house they were sitting in were dashed for the Will sisters. Avis took the disappointment better than expected; Elizabeth worse, even though they both knew it had been the kind of long shot only suckers bet. They were, after all, their father's daughters.

And apparently Frank had not come by his larcenous nature by accident.

The third document in the stapled batch was a fraudulent lease, authorized by a Thomas Will in 1880 just one year before his death. Frank's Great-great-grandmother Lydia's husband had—on the basis of the King's nullified grant and alleged hundred years of uninterrupted Will occupancy—leased almost all of Cap's Island to the Episcopal Church for $5,000—a considerable sum in 1880, for which the church had the right to construct whatever buildings its members saw fit, and to retain use of the land until 1980. It was quite a coup. According to the dates, Lydia had buried her husband, packed her things, and moved back to the mainland before the hotel could be completed, with no one the wiser.

Except the compiler of the documents: the man with the gun in the Children of Deity library. The man who had found a copy of the deed of sale from the Episcopal Diocese to a Pentecostal mission for the hotel in 1942, and the transferral to Garrett Selby twenty years later.

It was not until much later that they noticed the spiky pencil scrawl on the back of the deed copy. The note read, "1839 reversal of terms."

"What the hell does *that* mean?" Avis asked the ceiling.

"Probably that one of our forebears was paroled for good behavior," Elizabeth answered with a frown, half believing it.

"Ha, ha." Avis snatched up the papers and looked long and hard at the first page. "I think I've got it." She positioned the paper under Elizabeth's nose. "The inhabitancy condition. This whole area was thrown into an economic depression that lasted for decades after the War of 1812. Most of the islands were virtually abandoned until after the Civil War. I'll bet the Wills came back to the mainland for at least some part of that time and voided the grant."

"Which," Elizabeth reminded Avis, "was nullified in 1812 anyway."

"Oh, who cares? There's no way to prove it, one way or the other, even if it mattered, which it doesn't."

Elizabeth chewed on her thumbnail. "Except it might. And we do have documentation of inhabitancy."

"Where?"

"In the family Bible that's disappeared so damned suddenly."

"Mother might know," Avis said.

Elizabeth looked at her sister as though she were brain-dead. "Right. Maybe the Bible and Mom are together." Avis did not respond. She and Elizabeth were both wondering what their father was up to this time. And they both had the feeling that somehow Al Jenness had known.

The thundering of Frank's truck's exhaust system alerted Petunia, who scrambled to take her post at the kitchen door. Frank's two daughters waited behind the dog with less enthusiasm.

Frank pushed past his welcoming committee looking depleted and sallow. Out of habit he tossed Petunia a dog biscuit from the cookie jar and threw his jacket and Stetson on the kitchen table. Elizabeth was in no mood to put up a front of normality.

"Where the hell have you been? It's the middle of the night and Avis and I have been worried sick."

"As a matter of fact, your boyfriend Jesse got himself snagged up in someone's halibut trawl, and needed some medical attention."

"And where did *that* happen?" Elizabeth demanded.

"I've been out, *Mother*," he answered caustically. "Where, is none of your business. Is there anything to eat around here?"

"There's lobster stew in the freezer," Avis offered despite herself. Frank opened the freezer, removed a Tupperware bowl, and placed it in the microwave.

"We went out after you, Dad," Elizabeth persisted. "We caught up with Jesse's boat anchored off the north side of Cap's, but we never found you two. You weren't in the water diving, as you would have liked us to believe. Where the hell were you?"

Frank punched the cooking time into the microwave and started it. "I believe I told you that's none of your business. I believe I also told you to stay away from Cap's. Am I going to have to take the keys away from you?"

"We were worried," Avis defended herself and her sister.

"Well, stop." Frank was pulling the man-of-stone routine that used to drive Sal to throwing around the cast-iron cookware in frustration.

Elizabeth was more of a full-frontal-assault kind of woman. "You weren't in the water and you weren't at the hotel."

Frank turned his back on the fascinating microwave carousel and glared at her. "How would you know, Elizabeth?"

"Because we ended up being held at gunpoint inside the hotel by some trigger-happy thug because you couldn't leave a *note,* thank you. What were we supposed to do? Shrug our shoulders and say, 'Well, I guess they drowned,' and head back to shore? Of course we had to take a look at the island—for all we knew you and Jesse could have been boiling up mussels for lunch, or washed up on the rocks. The religious nut with the gun gave us a whole lot more to think about, unfortunately. But," Elizabeth continued, unwilling to give her father the chance to interrupt her tirade, "before we got away, I managed to get my hands on some papers that have to make me wonder what you haven't told us about the quagmire that is the Will gene pool." She threw the boosted papers on top of Frank's jacket and hat on the table. "We're over twenty-one, Dad. What's going on that you're not telling us?" Her father's reaction would tell her a lot about the course she was taking. One: he would laugh at her stupidity, or, two: he would 'fess up.

Or, three: he would completely lose control and frighten his children half to death. Which is exactly what he did.

He started slowly. "You went onto Cap's Island after I expressly forbade it? *Both* of you?" He crushed in his hand the papers Elizabeth had thrown on the table as his face turned purple with rage. Words chased one another as though shot from an automatic weapon. "Understand this: that island is death for us, *death*. Not a peaceful sleep, but horrible, painful, screaming death. It's a haunted place gorged with the bodies of our family and I *will not* let another Will rot in the ground because of a miserable piece of *rock*."

Avis, fearful that her father would have a heart attack right on the spot, reached out for his arm, but he shook her off furiously.

"*No.*" He held up his fist, the crushed paper white between his tightly balled fingers. "Papers don't mean anything. *You* mean something. And if I ever hear of either one of you within one hundred feet of that accursed hellhole, I swear I will bury you in the back woods with Lydia and never speak of you again." He turned his back and slammed into his bedroom. Petunia cowered beneath the sideboard.

Tears ran from the corners of Avis's eyes. A muscle twitched in Elizabeth's jaw.

"What are we going to do, Liz?" Avis ran her shirt-sleeve under her nose. "He's crazier than a shithouse rat."

"Bake some of that banana nut bread I love, keep your hands busy, and make sure Dad doesn't leave here without you." Elizabeth slid her arms into her father's discarded jacket.

"Where are you going?"

"To make Jesse spill his guts." Elizabeth opened the kitchen door. "And if he won't, I'll spill them for him, literally or figuratively. I don't give a damn."

For all his threats, Frank had left the keys to his truck in the ignition. She'd take the truck; if he decided to come after her, he would never be able to get the MGB on the road.

She tore into Jesse's driveway so fast and with so much screeching of brakes that the lights went on in the houses on both sides of the saltbox colonial. Jesse's lights were already on, not that she cared if she woke him.

She pulled the emergency brake so hard she wondered if she would ever be able to disengage it, slammed the truck door, and marched up the stairs to the storm door emblazoned with an ornate aluminum "K." She kicked the metal twice by way of knocking and stormed inside.

Jesse was sunk deep, head back and eyes closed, in a chintz-covered easy chair set a few feet from the dark television. He was fingering a heavy silver chain and circleted antique coin with one hand. The other hand was propped on the right arm of the chair, wrapped in surgical tape and gauze, blood moons showing under the fingernails. He *had* been hurt during the afternoon's travails, but God only knew how.

Startled, Jesse jumped up, wincing as he carelessly pressed his injured hand against the arm of the chair.

"Elizabeth!"

She rushed to the maple dining room set near the kitchen door and knocked every book, several pencils, and the salt and pepper set and matching sugar bowl to the braided rug with an adrenaline-fueled sweep of her arm.

"What's going on, Jesse? What were you and Dad up to this afternoon, and what is it that you're not telling me?"

"Nothing," Jesse protested indignantly.

"Bullshit." Elizabeth picked up one of the four maple captain's chairs and slammed it down hard enough to crack one of the crossbars. "Avis and I found the grant Dad's been hiding. I can't believe *you*, Mr. Historian, didn't know anything about it." Jesse remained frozen; Elizabeth believed she'd hit a nerve. "Then we got some supporting documents out of the library on Cap's Island." Jesse's eyes widened, but he did not trust himself to speak. "And almost got ourselves shot as trespassers for our trouble." That unglued the big man.

"You gotta stay off Cap's, Liz."

"Why, Jess? Why do I *have* to? Are there still too many people alive who've been defrauded over that miserable pile? Is that what's driven Dad crazy?"

"No!" Perspiration ran down Jesse's unshaven cheeks and into the neck of his sweatshirt. "Your father's not crazy, don't say such things, Liz; he's not crazy!"

"There's a man dead, Jess, and my mother is missing. Maybe she's dead, too. I don't know how to explain that except that it all has something to do with a shady land deal from a thousand years ago. Everything points to it. So my family is a bunch of crooks, and now murder."

"That's not true, Liz. You saw the papers." Jesse's eyebrows compressed, leaving a deep crease over the bridge of his nose. He was breathing hard, making a small grunting noise with each exhalation. He was struggling to find a way to turn away Elizabeth's assault, but she could smell blood.

"So Al Jenness knew the religious group on Cap's was taken for a ride—leased *state* land by Thomas Will in 1880—and Dad killed him to protect the family *honor*?"

Jesse's head swung from side to side in confusion. "I don't understand. You saw the papers. There was no fraud. Frank wouldn't kill Al because of the island; he could have held up construction of the casinos until hell freezes over."

"How, Jesse?"

Comprehension spread over Jesse's face and then evaporated. "Which papers did you see?"

Elizabeth, at the end of her tether, raised her hand in a crimson fury to slap the words from Jesse's mouth, but his reflexes were faster than hers. He easily caught her open right hand with his uninjured left. He could feel her trembling, and he could feel a physical ache in his heart.

"What's the bottom line, Jess? Please."

"The 1839 nullification, Lizzie. The United States nullified its own proclamation of 1812 that rescinded all land grants from the King."

Elizabeth slumped and supported herself on the edge of the table. "What are you saying, Jesse? That we still own Cap's Island?"

Jesse looked ill. He lifted his pouch of tobacco, laid a rolling paper on the table, poured out a measure, and rolled a cigarette without difficulty. He pulled his trusty Zippo from his left pocket and lit the end.

"Not you." Jesse exhaled a billow of smoke into the room. "Frank owns it, maybe."

"Maybe?"

Jesse nodded miserably.

Garrett Selby stood waiting in the parlor of Will's Cottage. He stood in the dark room and watched the moon slide from its two o'clock position to four. His brother had been out of the cottage for at least an hour and a half. When Eli slunk in, Garrett rotated on the balls of his feet to face the door. As the light switch was flipped up, Eli gasped.

"Jesus."

Garrett grimaced. "Do not, on top of everything else, take the Lord's name in vain, Eli."

"Fuck you," Eli drawled, and walked to his bedroom. "What are you doing here in the middle of the night anyway? Getting impure thought vibes coming from this direction?" He kicked out of his sodden athletic shoes and stripped off his wet clothes. Cold to his bones, he turned the knobs in the shower stall to hot and stepped in. Garrett remained standing and patient until the water stopped running and Eli was toweled off and in a robe.

"I know what you've been doing, Eli."

"Cleanliness is next to godliness, brother," Eli sniped and poured himself a glass of Scotch.

"You have been lusting," Garrett continued, undaunted by Eli's sarcasm. "You have been lusting and coveting." He walked to the northeast bedroom window and looked across the water toward Piscatawk Island. "You are the man who has been frightening the women on the next island. You are a Peeping Tom, Eli," he accused.

Garrett swallowed his Scotch. "That would make me a Peeping Eli, then, wouldn't it? Besides, you know I can't swim."

"I do know that. I also found out this afternoon how you get onto Piscatawk without a boat and without having to swim a stroke. You walk."

Eli poured another measure of liquor into his glass. "On water! Hallelujah, brother. It's a *miracle.*" Garrett lunged at his heretical brother and slapped the tumbler from his hand. Eli smiled benevolently. "I forgive you. I know what a strain it must be, knowing that you're comforting your flock in someone else's field." Eli sucked a mouthful of Scotch directly from the neck of the bottle. "The jig is up, Garrett, and so is your lease, but the prodigal son might just have bought you a little time."

"I don't know what you're talking about."

"Sure you do," Eli smirked. "Bait and switch, big brother. Bait and switch."

Elizabeth coasted the noisy truck to the front of the gallery so that its return would be unheard by her sister, her father, or the occasionally vigilant Petunia. The dog was accustomed to customers parking all over the place during the summers and did not raise a row over the sound of Elizabeth's shoes on the gravel.

The sun had risen over the horizon enough that she could find her way to the barn doors without tripping over anything. She lifted the left door to keep it from grating over the rocky ground and moved it aside just enough to squeeze inside the cluttered barn. She reached down for the kerosene lamp that was kept just inside the door, but it had been moved, and she was forced to dig around in her pants pockets for the waterproof matches she always carried.

The match caught on its first trip across the rusty horseshoe over the door. The lantern was hung from a nail at hand level. Liz lifted the front casing and fired the wick. Greasy smoke drew a line to the ceiling.

Everything had been moved. Her father's time had been efficiently spent the day he cleaned out the old picture frames. There was a clear area ten by fifteen feet in the center of the barn that Elizabeth could not remember having seen before. The expanse was broken only by the impossibly heavy floor safe and a smattering of ancient hay that had fallen from the sagging hayloft along the left side of the building.

Frank's attack of neatness, which would have warmed Elizabeth's heart one week ago, sent a shudder down her back. Why? If she had had little idea where to begin her search before, she was completely stymied now. The safe that had previously been dumping its guts of ledgers and moldy receipts was now securely locked. As far as she knew, the combination had been lost about the time it had been moved to its present position.

Or had it? Numbers. She was wearing the same jeans she'd had on the day she caught Ginny searching the barn; she shoved her hands into the pockets and pulled out the numbers copied from Al Jenness's note. Not knowing which way to start, she chose left 17, right 65, left 12, right 39, left 80, and then all the way around the dial again to right 80. The door refused to open. Quickly she reversed the left-right order, placing her ear against the door to try to catch the sound of tumblers. Then she tried both again.

She'd almost fallen. Whatever Al was trying to say, it had nothing to do with the antiquated safe. Frank had cleaned the barn and shut up the safe so that Elizabeth would be convinced what she was looking for was locked away inside. Frank did not have the combination to reopen it any more than Petunia did.

Elizabeth dropped into a squat, balancing on her haunches and trying to crawl into her father's mind while she figured out which pieces of junk had ended up where. Without thinking, she picked up a long strand of dried grass and began to chew on it. She immediately spat it out and picked tiny pieces off her tongue with her fingers. The hay had taken on the unpleasant damp smell of the barn and, she saw as she looked down, had grown quite a crop of mold. Decades of compacting had blocked the flow of air that would have kept it dry. It negated the whole point of having a hayloft.

She looked up and considered. No hay had fallen out of the loft before because it was congealed into a mildewy lump. The only reason any had dislodged was because someone had been in the loft, and the only reason for someone to be up there would be to put something away. As long as the something was off the floor, the loft would be the driest place. And old books needed to be kept dry.

Petunia's barking jolted Elizabeth from her self-congratulatory reverie. The family was up. She would have to come back later to retrieve the Bible.

The barn door was pulled open behind her, but it was not her father or sister come to get her.

"Wanna come to the house, Biz?" Ginny asked from outside.

"This official?" Elizabeth asked her old friend.

" 'Fraid so."

"Be right there," Elizabeth promised, though she did not stand. Ginny allowed Elizabeth a moment to collect herself and walked alone up the drive to the house.

Elizabeth counted to three, got to her feet, and studied her route. The ladder was long gone; the huge spikes driven into the timbers would have to do. The loft was no more than ten feet up. She raised her knee as high as she could and planted the sole of her sneaker on the lowest of the oversized nails. Grasping a bracing board, she pulled herself up and found another foothold. In four contortions she was in the loft. Pigeons that had been nesting just inside the broken laths of the window vent flew off frantically, their wings making a *whoomph, whoomph* as they evacuated. To her right, Elizabeth could barely make out the black lumps of what she recognized as wasp nests hanging from the rafters: precisely the sort of daunting place Frank would choose to protect something as important as the family Bible.

Testing each pine floor plank carefully before she let her full weight down, Elizabeth made her way toward the wasps. Visions of her Aunt Arlene's stinging death buzzed through her mind's eye. *Insidious,* she thought. *Positively perverse.* A piece of plastic wrap poked out from a dark wall brace two inches from the largest of the nests. She had to reach for it. She tried to remember whether wasps vacated their nests during daylight and, if that was true, whether there was daylight enough. She had to hurry. Ginny wasn't about to leave her alone for long.

Elizabeth took a deep breath and, trying to keep her hand as tightly folded and compact as possible, reached for the plastic-wrapped volume. Her hand brushed the black thing suspended from the ceiling and she froze in primitive revulsion.

The inky form was warm.

But then, everyone knows bats are warm-blooded. And nocturnal. Elizabeth's final pull at the book dislodged it along with one of the hanging bat's feet. She could see a baby bat clutching its mother's stomach while the adult bat pawed sleepily and reconnected with the rafter.

Rather than waste more time squirreling her way back to the ground floor, Liz tucked the Bible into her shirt and jumped from the loft. Her knees complained but did not pop. She went to the rear of her fractious MGB to lay the Bible atop the sagging double muffler, then back to the house, where the police were waiting. Not just Ginny, but Mr. Elwell the summer cop and two men borrowed from the nearby Hampton department.

"I called Jesse, Liz," Avis said the moment Elizabeth entered, "and he's going to raise bail and meet Dad at the station. Dad insisted, but I called Gerald in Virginia, too."

"Always said we needed a lawyer in the family," Frank commented dryly.

"Are you arresting Dad?" Elizabeth asked Ginny.

"Already has," Frank answered. "Got my rights 'n' everything. Did a damned good job, Ginny. Gonna cuff me?" Ginny shook her head and, avoiding Elizabeth's eyes, walked Frank out to the police cruiser as the backup cops started going through the house.

Frank ordered over his shoulder to his daughters, "You two stay here and make sure those Neanderthals don't make a mess of our decor." Ginny shut the passenger door, got in, and backed the cruiser down the hill.

"The search warrant is in order," Avis admitted unhappily. "I checked."

"Figured it would be," Elizabeth said. "C'mon. Let's go get some breakfast." She went to the hall and asked Mr. Elwell, "That okay?"

"Sure. We'll be careful, I promise."

Avis balked. "I don't want to go for breakfast. I think I'm going to barf as it is. Besides, Dad asked us to stay here."

"Dad asks for a lot of things. Now, I want breakfast. Do I have to beat you up to get you to come along?"

Avis thought that would be regressive and followed her sister out the door. Avis had to push the MGB two hundred yards down the road before it would start, and then had to hunch above on the family Bible all the way to the Athenaeum in the next town.

"I thought you wanted breakfast," Avis said, shifting uncomfortably on the book in the bucket seat. "What do you expect to find at the Athenaeum?"

"1839." Elizabeth downshifted and lost one of the loose mufflers. She watched it clatter away in the rearview mirror, finding its final resting place on the soft shoulder. "But I don't know if I want to use it or not," she shouted above the booming of the sports car's exhaust.

EIGHTEEN

THE THREE-STORY white clapboard Town Hall in the center of Dovekey Beach was filled. The League of Women Voters' refreshment table was picked nearly clean, the coffee already scorched in the five-gallon electric urns, the piddly business that is always addressed at such gatherings such as running dogs and removal of road kill debated in stultifying detail. The final vote—the one that everyone had turned out for—was about to be called. Ginny Philbrick leaned inside the double doors to the chambers and worried. It was showtime and several of the leading players were absent.

Judge Spirou had set what Ginny considered an incredibly low bail for Frank, which Jesse covered as immediately as could only happen in a town where the police station, judge's quarters *cum* courthouse, and savings and loan were located on a stretch of road no longer than an average city block. Frank should have been back home before the Hampton police completed the search of his house and barn, which had turned up nothing more than the fact that the house could use some fresh paint and wallpaper. But neither Frank nor Jesse was present to rabble-rouse in opposition to the proposal for legalized gambling and prostitution. Almost more worrisome was the fact that Elizabeth and her sister were also missing.

Garrett Selby stood apart from the townspeople, which was difficult in the crowded space, but that was precisely where he believed himself to belong. He could not help glaring at Ruth Jenness, seated on the dais in her late husband's place. She had taken his place in several ways, of course, but no one else in the room knew that except Selby. He tried to find it in his heart to forgive the woman her ungodly greed, but failed.

Asa Fleck motioned for the vote and Maggie seconded the motion. Vinnie Bartlett called for discussion, hoping that without Frank and Elizabeth, there would not be much—he had to be at the Breakfast 'n' Beans by four-thirty in the morning to do his prep work and did not think a lot of jabbering was going to change anyone's mind at this late date.

The voters of Dovekey Beach shifted in their folding chairs and looked around for the citizens most likely to pick up the gauntlet. No one rose to the occasion. Ginny caught Sandy's eye. Sandy shrugged and finished the last bite of one of Edith Ryan's famous cinnamon doughnuts. Vinnie waited nearly another minute for someone to speak up. When no one did, he called for a show of hands. If the sides split at all evenly, the question would go to a written ballot and severely shorten his night's sleep.

Ginny quickly stepped to the outside stairs to see if any latecomers were pulling in. The road was deserted in the evening gloom. A light fog had rolled in off the water, saturating the air with moisture and the smell of salt and freshly turned seaweed.

Vinnie cleared his throat and asked, "All those in favor of passing the ordinance allowing gaming establishments and state-regulated brothels on offshore islets within the jurisdiction of the Township of Dovekey Beach?"

Hands shot up, and Maggie Fleck scribbled furiously in her steno pad. Garrett Selby lifted his chin slightly and made his way toward the door.

Ginny stepped back inside the hall to register her vote, but remained close to the exit in case there was trouble, thinking it was probably best that Elizabeth not know that her best friend in the world was against her pet legislation.

"Opposed?"

On his way to the parking lot, Selby nodded to Ginny as she raised her hand. Vinnie smiled in relief. The B 'n' B would be doing a landslide business the next morning, and he would be well rested. No need for a ballot that night.

The copy machine at the Athenaeum was broken. Avis tried to look on the bright side: neither she nor Elizabeth had a dime between them anyway to feed into the antiquated machinery. Elizabeth managed without too much difficulty to bully the curator into letting them remove the one book they needed on the promise they would return it the next morning. The ferocious brightness of the Newington Mall would be a welcome respite from the dusty piles of delicate volumes and the darkened microfiche viewing rooms. In addition, duplicates at the Copies R Hank shop were only a nickel, and there was no waiting line.

Unfortunately, it took an hour and a half more before AAA showed up in the expansive mall parking lot to hook up the booster cables on the MGB. The drive back to the Cape Cod house in Dovekey Beach took longer than the usual fifteen minutes because of the way the MGB's headlights faded in and out all along the winding beach road. Avis did not entirely understand Elizabeth's snapping temper, despite all these complications. They had found what they'd been searching for. It was Elizabeth who insisted that they each have a copy of every document and made them miss the Town Meeting.

Elizabeth downshifted to pull into the driveway; the sports car stalled at the entrance. She and Avis easily pushed the dead vehicle into the gallery parking space between Avis's Jeep and Frank's truck.

"What do you think he's going to say?" Avis asked, handing Elizabeth the borrowed book and stack of copies.

"I have no idea," Elizabeth answered and handed the book back to her sister. "You take your copies and the book home. I don't want any more of these papers wandering."

"You're not going to talk to him without me." Avis held the book aloft. "The reversal of 1839 reestablished our right to Cap's Island. I want to see his face when we tell him."

"I think he already knew about it. Why else would he hide the family Bible? If the condition of inhabitancy was not met, then Cap's reverted to the state more than one hundred years ago."

Avis looked fragile in the moonlight. "So, you think Dad's opposition to the gambling bill is because he plans to make a claim on the island? Why? He hates the place. If the state takes it for conversion to a casino complex, we'll be paid a fortune and he'll be free of it." She rethought her position. "But if we don't have any right to the island, then he's been telling the truth all along." Her face brightened. "Maybe he didn't even know there was a chance that Cap's was ours."

"Maybe. Maybe not. But Al Jenness knew, so it can't be all that secret." Elizabeth handed her sister the paper with the numbers dashed off in Ginny's handwriting. "This is a list of the applicable dates regarding the title. One, seven, six, five is 1765, the date of the charter. Then they run chronologically. One, two, is twelve for 1812, the date of the nullification. Three-nine is 1839, the federal proclamation reinstituting land grants. The two eighties at the end must be for the year the land was leased to the church and the year the lease expires.

"I don't know why Dad hid the Bible, but I know he did, and whatever's in there may negate our claim to Cap's. There's still a piece of the puzzle missing. Mom was always fascinated with that Bible, and now she's missing. I want you to go home."

"No." Avis slammed the car door. The sound rang like a shot over the rhythmic whirring of crickets.

"It's most important that you get those papers to a safe place, Avis." Elizabeth moved between her sister and the house. She was backlit by the porch light, and Avis could not make out the expression on her face. "I'm not going to say anything to Dad about what we found tonight."

"Promise?"

"Cross my heart and hope to die, stick a needle in my eye." Elizabeth invoked the age-old childhood pledge. Avis smiled despite herself.

"Okay, then, if you promise." She opened the door to her Jeep and got in. "But I'll be back first thing tomorrow morning, and we'll get to the bottom of this together. Right?"

"Right." Elizabeth shut the Jeep's door and waved. As soon as Avis had pulled out of sight, she tossed the Copies R Hank bag through the open window and onto the front seat of the MGB, and marched up the slope to confront her father.

Needles in eyes notwithstanding.

Town Hall cleared out quickly. The gravel parking area was empty, the one halogen streetlamp turning the powder-blue police cruiser almost silvery.

"I can't believe it," Sandy said from the passenger seat. "I thought the vote would be *close*, at least. Jeez. Frank's going to be pretty upset."

"Frank's got bigger fish to fry," Ginny said, starting the motor and steering the cruiser away from the center of town.

"Where are we going?" Sandy asked as they headed in the opposite direction from their apartment.

"Just a quick patrol," Ginny answered.

Five minutes later they passed the Will house. The first-floor lights were on and Frank's and Elizabeth's vehicles were parked in front of the gallery. Ginny let out an involuntary sigh of relief, did a U-turn in the middle of the deserted road, and looked forward to a good night's sleep.

Good as his word, Frank had taken his truck keys with him, wherever that was. Elizabeth threw the dog two biscuits, discovered the spare set missing from where she kept them on her bureau, and slammed the back door with more determination than ever, thanking her higher power that a few years with the MGB had made her the hot-wire expert of Dovekey Beach, New Hampshire.

The truck turned over at the first spark. One headlight was burned out, but the night was bright enough that it did not much matter in the two miles to the mooring. Without surprise, Elizabeth observed the dory bobbing at the *Celia T.*'s mooring. She thought she could hear the pulse in her throat as she rowed out to the *Curmudgeon,* tied up, and boarded. Without her father on board to help, the double air tank fought her, but she managed to land it on the rail without damage.

Frank had not found the spare set of keys she had hidden for both their sakes under the marine radio.

The fog was low-lying, wafting only a foot above the water. She passed the beacon from Whaleback light to the left of the harbor, feeling fortunate that she could navigate by sight. For all her time on the ocean, she had never learned to steer by the stars, and the *Curmudgeon* had limited (to say the least) technological advances.

As the lobster boat pulled within a mile of the islands, Elizabeth threw the engine into neutral, doused the lights, and stripped off her clothes. The fog condensed immediately on her bare skin and wet her underwear before she could cover herself with a thick skin of baby powder. The talc lumped in a paste as she powdered the inside of the wet suit. Rolling the black rubberized jumpsuit over her body was more difficult because of her unpredictable shudders. Once she was encased, the shivering ceased, and she was able to maneuver the craft past where Al Jenness's body had been retrieved and wide around the eastern tip of Piscatawk.

Newly installed floodlights glared at the dock entrance but did not reach the slow-moving vessel. The ocean-facing side of the islands remained as dark as the strident moon would allow. Nonetheless, the dark green enamel that clothed the *Celia T.* camouflaged her more effectively on the quiet water between Piscatawk and Cap's islands than Elizabeth would have imagined.

There was no pretense of a diving expedition for Frank and Jesse that night: no diver's flag or buoy. She'd known there wouldn't be. Frank's scuba equipment was stashed on the shelf of his bedroom closet back home and he was too thick to fit into one of Jesse's spares.

Liz coasted into position behind the *Celia T.* and dropped anchor with as little splash as she could manage. As additional insurance, she tossed a loop over one of the chrome T-hooks on the rail of the other boat and secured the two vessels to each other. She spit into the faceplate of her rubber mask, double-checked the regulator on the air tank, and swished the mask in the water over the side. Adjusting the faceplate, she slid feet first into the water.

The darkness beneath the night sea was black as death.

The yellow rubber raft lay smothered in kelp at the rocky shallows on the north side of Cap's Island. The hotel and caretaker's cottage had closed their eyes for the night, shades pulled against the invasive moon, sleeping the sleep of the righteous. Though they were somewhat hidden by the crest of the small hill, the two men stayed low to the ground and made their way into the rubble of the collapsed building. Jesse turned his back to the Children of Deity hotel, pulled away a crosshatching of weathered wood, and switched on the flashlight. The shattered body of a three-foot marble cherub lay sprawled in the circle of light. Frank lowered himself on both knees and scooped debris a foot in either direction. The marble base was broken into two pieces. With his pocket knife he dug out the lettering. Even with the break in the middle, Frank could read the inscription:

ONE HUNDRED YEARS WE TITHE THE CROWN,
ALIVE OR STILL.
HEREWITH PROOF OUR PLEDGE TO THE NAME OF WILL.

The dull slapping of the waves against the shoreline was eerily unrelenting without the covering sounds of daylight birds.

"So?" Frank asked without emotion.

Jesse was taken aback. "This is your island, Frank," he whispered earnestly. "This is Will's Island. Underneath all this junk is the Will burial plot. Here"—Jesse dug with his hands, sweeping away dried seaweed, gravel, and wood debris until he came across a forearm's length of milled granite—"the tombstones are here under the old servants' quarters. Lots of them."

"I'll bet," Frank commented. "We're a fertile bunch. So, what's your point, Jesse?"

"This is *your* island, Frank," Jesse explained again eagerly. "I found all the papers to prove it. The only thing that was missing was the provision that Wills live on this island every year for a hundred years from 1765 until 1865. Your Gramma Lydia's husband was buried here in 1880. That proves it."

"No, Jess," Frank said kindly. "It only proves that Grampa Tom was buried here in that year."

Jesse's brow furrowed. "Good enough for me." Frank simply shook his head sadly. "Good enough for a lot of people, Frank," Jesse persisted. "That hotel there belongs to you. Only the land was leased, and that lease ran out years ago. It's *yours* and *Lizzie's*."

"How do you know that, Jess?" Frank asked. Jesse looked around in a quandary. Frank was supposed to be thrilled with the news, but he did not act as though he were. Jesse looked to the ocean for the answer, but all he got was a glimpse of the bow of the *Curmudgeon* sneaking from behind the *Celia T.*

"Shit."

"Jesse, answer me."

"Frank"—Jesse pointed seaward—"Lizzie's out here."

Frank looked in the direction of Jesse's finger and saw his boat lashed to Jesse's. No one else could have brought her out to the islands. Heedless of danger, Frank rose to his full height and ran to the hidden raft, Jesse barely jumping into the aft as Frank pushed out toward where he prayed his elder daughter was waiting to berate him.

If she was not lying in wait on the boat, he would rather she was snagged in the razor wire on Piscatawk than have her set one foot on Cap's.

Time and distance were suspended in the enveloping ink of the water. Elizabeth tried to keep about ten feet below the surface, pumping her swim fins in a long, slow rhythm, her hands thrust palms forward to avoid propelling herself face first into any submerged rock. She knew she was taking in air too quickly, but the fear of swimming blind prevented her from breathing regularly. She imagined the bubbles from her tanks hitting the surface in huge explosions and inhaled and exhaled even more rapidly.

She wondered if too much oxygen was making her see a lightening in the water. She pushed down another two feet and spotted rocks beneath her—almost impossible to see in the dark but, still, rising toward her belly. She realized she must be nearing shore and pulled herself by her hands along the rocks and shells on the bottom. Her head broke the surface with a minimum of splash. She was not even sure which island she was on.

In fact, she had surfaced on neither island, but between the two, slightly nearer Cap's. It was more than curious. Everything she understood about the topography of the islands told her that they rose steeply from underwater cliffs. There would be no gradual incline as there was toward shore on the mainland. She groped beneath the water's surface to her right and then to her left and remembered that one of the first things her father had taught her when she started fishing with him was that it was too shallow to navigate between the two larger islands. She had never questioned why.

She reached forward and pushed. She floated three feet in the direction of the mainland and reached down. The shallow water ended and her arm could not reach bottom. Turning back until she could trace the shallows with her fingers, she followed the line of submerged rocks to Piscatawk. The reason the waters were calm between the two islands was because a breakwater had been built at some time in the past. Two, actually. Elizabeth remembered that the grant identified Will's Island as lying south and east at the breakwater from Smith's. The three islands had been joined at one time. The shifting ocean had submerged the man-made barriers, but with the gravitational pull of the full moon, the water had receded enough that she could have walked on them, albeit almost up to her knees in the cold salt water.

In fact, that is what the man watching her from the east shore of Cap's was expecting her to do. Second-guessing Elizabeth Will was the most amusement the man had had in some time. He crossed his arms and enjoyed himself.

The man-made granite bridge ended at the low side of Piscatawk, putting Elizabeth face to face with a cloud of Dr. Charles MacKay's precious razor wire. Slipping off her swim fins, Elizabeth knelt on the sunken wall cap and slowly stood. Hardly stretching, she stepped over MacKay's primitive security and faced the backs of the stark dormitories about five hundred yards away. Disgusted with herself, she thought of the twin crucified seagulls. One on her bed, one at the window that must watch from the building ahead. Her father with access to both places.

She found herself walking to the outbuilding, the soft foam of her diving boots cushioning each step, making the trek seem even more unreal. One opened window in one dorm faced north and west; the sea grass beneath had been trampled flat by multiple feet. *This must be the room,* Elizabeth thought. She peered through the window into the small bedroom. On the floor, next to the bunk, sat a stone marker. Her head jerked to one side, eyes rejecting what they read. She wished she had brought a flashlight as she bent double and slipped through the window. Her boots made her entrance absolutely silent, though she imagined an almost imperceptible squooshing as she crossed the linoleum floor and lifted the marker. From the moonlight at the window she made out the inscription.

ELIZABETH WILL

Her own tombstone was leaden in her hands.

Repulsed, Elizabeth heaved the evil thing out the window, and while a crawling shiver worked its way from the small of her back up to her shoulders, she was jerked violently three feet off the floor and hurled to the metal bed.

The *Curmudgeon* was as deserted as a ghost ship, the inflatable life-raft snug in its heavy-gauge oilskin pouch Velcroed to the forward door, an abandoned snorkel hose on the deck. Jesse gaped in disbelief.

Without hesitating, Frank pulled on his rubberized coveralls, which ended in heavy boots. "Get in the raft, Jesse. You look for her on Cap's, and I'll search Piscatawk."

"You'll never be able to land the inflatable on Piscatawk, Frank. The razor wire'll rip her to shreds."

"I'm not taking the inflatable, Jess," Frank said, pushing off and rowing for all he was worth. "We'll beach on Cap's and I'll walk the breakwater."

"You know about that?"

" 'Twas my great-great-great-grandfather that paid for it. Guess the hell I know." Jesse's back was to the island. All Frank's concentration was on pulling the oars as smoothly through the water as he could manage. Neither man noticed the dark shape walking on water.

"Frank, you shouldn't wear those coveralls. If'n you slip, them boots is gonna fill with water and sink you to the bottom before you can say hell." The front of the raft hit the rock shore. Jesse jumped out and pulled the boat onto land.

"Not gonna slip, Jess," Frank said, already twenty feet nearer the breakwater, his trip made faster by the light newly shining from Will's Cottage on his left.

The scuba mask was jammed into the crook of Elizabeth's throat. Her head tilted forward sharply against the oversoft mattress, and her chest was frighteningly compressed by the heavy man on her back. Just as she thought her ribs would collapse simultaneously with the crushing of her trachea, she was wrenched off the cot and dragged to the doorway. The man's grasp was made more vise-like with the traction of the spongy wet suit. She was allowed one gasp of air before a hairy forearm was slapped about her neck and the lights flashed on. The hood of her diving suit was ripped off over her face, taking with it a good bit of strawberry-blond hair. Her captor threw her to the floor.

Charles MacKay looked down on Elizabeth with the wrath of an unshaven, sleep-deprived god.

"You!" he accused. "You?" he questioned either himself or her. She could not be sure; she was still trying to suck air into her burning lungs.

"Where's my father?" she demanded, so afraid of the answer that she blustered.

MacKay paused, thrown for a loop. He'd been sure he had caught his peeper; now he seemed to have the peeper's daughter.

"You tell me," he ordered, buying himself some time.

"I don't know, dammit. He's out here somewhere with Jesse Kneeland. The boat's anchored just off Cap's."

"Then why didn't you look there?"

"I don't know," she answered feebly. Because she was forbidden to go to Cap's by the man she was looking for? Because she was fascinated by her discovery of a stupid breakwater? "How did you know I was in here?" she asked.

"I was waiting; you walked in. Simple. We've been putting up with your—or your father's—fun and games for too long. Chief Philbrick didn't have any suggestions, so I took the bull by the horns, if you will." MacKay could not help noticing how—for lack of a better word—*healthy* Elizabeth Will looked wet. A two-second grapple with his libido returned him to his perpetually angry state. "Get out of that wet suit and hand it to me through the door so I can count on your still being here after I call the police." He would post the water boy outside in case Big Frank Will showed up for his nightly peep. "Wrap yourself in a blanket or something if you're cold," he added without wanting to. He did not care if she got cold.

MacKay waited in the hall with his arm stuck through the crack of the door. Boots, vest, and then pants piled on top of the hood he had already removed. He kicked them aside, locked the door, and trudged to the maintenance director's office to call Ginny Philbrick to get her ass out to the island and collect her prisoner.

Elizabeth's underwear was soaked and the room was cold, but she could not bring herself to be completely naked in the strange bedroom. The closet revealed itself as desolately empty, with the exception of a Boston Red Sox cap and one sock. Her teeth began to chatter, so she broke down and took MacKay's suggestion, bundling herself in a white thermal blanket she pulled off the small bed before inspecting the three small dresser drawers.

The top drawer contained a few orphaned photographs, one of a shirtless Dr. Charles MacKay. Elizabeth blew a short burst of air from her lungs, threw the packet back, and moved to the next. Empty. She reopened the first drawer and took another glance at what a Ph.D. looks like stripped to the waist. She sat on the bed, drained by fear and exertion, and closed her eyes for a few moments. She opened them on the photo of MacKay, blew another puff of appreciative air, and redoubled her efforts to cover herself.

The bottom drawer yielded one Columbia University Old Blue Rugby Club T-shirt, size extra large. She held it up to check the length. *Obviously rugby players' extra larges are larger than human extra larges.* The shirt covered her to mid-thigh. MacKay was efficient; judging by the size of the complex, he would be back in her face any minute, and she still had not found her father.

Elizabeth turned the shirt right side out, braced herself for the cold, and dropped her blanket. She had both arms in the sleeves and the neck poised over her head when she was hit from behind. Her first instinct was that MacKay was back, but then she reasoned that her attacker had come from the window side of the room. MacKay could have simply opened the door. Without the impediment of the wet suit, Elizabeth found herself much more efficient at self-defense.

The shirt and a large hand muffled her shouts. The T-shirt blinded her, but she raised her heel in a burst of strength she had not known she still possessed and kicked toward her buttocks. She caught the man in the testicles, causing him to let out a bellow of pain and rage before he stumbled backward, releasing her to pull the shirt down and turn to see her attacker. She saw Eli Selby flattened like a June bug against the windowsill.

Around Eli's throat was an elbow she knew as well as her own.

From where he crouched outside Debra's bedroom, Frank had Selby throttled.

MacKay was glad he had returned with a weapon.

As far as Jesse could tell, no one was up and around on Cap's Island. The hotel was completely dark, except for a desk lamp that had been left on in the library. The front door was unlocked and he slipped easily into the foyer and down the hall to the source of the light. He listened cautiously at the door for a moment and then let himself in. Reverend Selby must have retired with the rest of the community.

The leather-topped desk was immaculate. Even the one book that rested on its surface was marked neatly with a bookmark and aligned dead center. The binding was worn in a way that Jesse's self-trained eye recognized as being caused by daily use over many years. He could not resist.

It was a journal, not the religious tract he had expected. But it had been painstakingly written over four decades by a man of the cloth, Parson Nathaniel Brackett. The page that appeared beneath the needlepoint bookmark was dated November 9, 1840, and read:

> *This day of our Lord we layd to rest the childe Elizabeth Will, beloved daughter of Thomas and Lydia. Mistress Lyddy was sore bereaved and my poor attempts to comfort her were met with scorn. Her husband was full aware of their blessing in young Josiah, but Mistress Lydia remains inconsolable. I fear their decision to await the childe four months hence on the mainland will become their way and we will loose yet another fine family from this isle. I will pray for the last of this olde family and the new babe, but have little hope for their return to us.*

Jesse dropped like a rock into the fine leather chair behind the desk. His head pounded as though every drop of blood in his body had rushed to a spot just between his eyes. Frank was right. His ancestors had left the islands in direct opposition to the codicil of the original grant. The island was forfeit.

Two more pages were noted, one reveling in Thomas and Lydia's return to Cap's Island with their new baby boy, John; and the occasion of twin births in 1870 to Josiah and Sarah Will of a healthy son and stillborn daughter, named Lydia for her grandmother. All the children were baptized by Pastor Brackett in the small church on the island.

Heart beating rapidly, Jesse went to the shelf of old books by the door of the library and found the huge old church records. Pastor Brackett had, indeed, recorded and dated each baptism.

Jesse returned the baptismal records to their place on the shelf, slipped the journal into his jacket pocket, and exited the front door without anyone having seen or heard him. As he made his way around the dark hotel in the direction of the inflatable raft, he saw the distinctive running lights of the Dovekey Beach Police skiff racing toward Piscatawk Island and passing another slower vessel. With no more care for secrecy, Jesse ran for the small rubber boat and launched for the Eternal Sea Group and whatever trouble waited there.

Frank had to admit that Eli Selby was cool under fire. Elizabeth admitted nothing of the sort. If Eli had seen something the night of Al Jenness's murder, he should have reported it.

MacKay admitted to himself that he never knew a rugby shirt could look so good, and poured everyone, including Eli—what the hell—a snifter of good cognac in hopes of coaxing some explanations from the tight-lipped natives. So Eli was the peeper, that was obvious; the man admitted it. He got past the sensors by wading carefully over the breakwater MacKay had never known existed, and was savvy enough about the fine points of the judicial system to hold out a bit of information for the local constabulary in trade for leniency. What kind of insidious history could the brother of a zealot missionary have, MacKay wondered.

Elizabeth sat back in a brown tweed Swedish modern armchair and stole glances at Eli and then MacKay. Then MacKay again, then Eli. The men had more in common than they realized. Gruff, unfinished. She crossed her legs at the knees where they were propped on the faux-pine coffee table. Eli watched. So did MacKay. Frank glowered at them both. Eli noticed. MacKay did not. Elizabeth wished Avis were with her almost as much as she wanted Ginny to arrive.

Debra ushered Jesse into the faculty lounge and exited in one smooth move. His large round face lit like a star at the sight of Elizabeth; his eyes were rimmed with red. *Bless him,* she thought. *There's something to be said for stolid, after all.* He walked to the side of her chair and squatted to examine her face.

"You okay, Lizzie?" She nodded and patted his cheek gratefully. She couldn't miss the wolfish grin that spread over Eli's face at her expression of affection. Her father had been essentially mute since body-slamming Eli against the wall, even when Elizabeth took him aside to challenge him with the proof she and Avis had located that Cap's Island belonged to the family. It was as though he had been stricken stone deaf.

Ginny and Garrett Selby entered the room arguing the continuation of a disagreement that had picked up on the Piscatawk dock from where it had left off at the town wharf at Dovekey Beach Harbor. Eli grinned once more; it never ceased to amuse the hell out of him when his brother was forced to defend him.

Garrett Selby finished a sentence as Ginny closed the door behind them with "We only have the one skiff on Cap's, Chief. One skiff. Our guests are brought out by tourist crafts exclusively— insurance, you know. My brother doesn't even know how to operate a water vehicle."

Which may or may not be true, Elizabeth reasoned, *but it doesn't matter. The church skiff is too unstable to have transported Al Jenness's body and the trap wrapped around it. The whole shebang would have capsized.*

"Chief Philbrick!" Eli saluted. "Glad you could make it for my confession."

"My pleasure," Ginny answered, wanting very much to know why Elizabeth was sitting around half naked in a rugby shirt. Instead of asking, she read Eli Selby his Miranda rights and took out a small pad of paper on which to take notes. "You want to confess to the whole ball of wax, or start small?"

"Before we get to what I'm guilty of, I'd like to know what kind of consideration I can expect for the exchange of information regarding the death of your selectman, What's-his-name."

Elizabeth sat forward and spat the name, "Al Jenness, you voyeur son of a bitch." Eli winked at her and Jesse squeezed her arm to prevent her from getting up and belting the suspect. MacKay poured another dollop of cognac into Elizabeth's snifter. Jesse wandered off by himself and fixed a very sweet, light coffee.

"Okay." Eli accepted Elizabeth's insult. "As an expression of good faith, I'll own up to that." He shrugged. "A misdemeanor at the worst."

"What else?" Ginny asked, fascinated by Eli's maneuvering. It was feeling a lot like New York again. "There must be more or you wouldn't be dangling the bait."

"I'm currently on probation, and the benevolent State of Massachusetts wouldn't mind putting me up for the summer at all."

"Thanks," said Ginny, writing. "For what?"

"A little of this, a little of that." Ginny flipped the notepad closed and pulled the handcuffs off her belt. "Okay, okay. Racketeering." From his lips it sounded almost like "jaywalking." "I was making some book, taking numbers, nothing big. I don't wanna go down for some dipshit beef with the ASPCA, you know?"

"The gulls were your idea of a prank?" Elizabeth shouted, seeing in her mind's eye her desecrated bed.

"Gull, babe, one gull." His eyes swept up and down her bare legs.

"I'll accept that," Ginny conceded.

"How can you, Gin?" Elizabeth challenged. "You saw both of them."

"I did, and they looked like totally different mutilations. The one that Bent-Nose here is admitting to was nailed live to a couple of driftwood sticks in the basic configuration of a cross." The Reverend Selby looked as though he would be sick on the pristine white tile floor, but held his tongue. "The other was a dried-out old thing that Dr. Ryan assures me was shot first with a thirty-eight, and—literally—hung around for weeks. The neck was broken sometime after death, and the pinfeathers shot to hell from the garroting and then nailed to oak lath."

Frank's face remained utterly placid.

Elizabeth was shocked. She should have noticed that peculiarity about the bird on the bed. Of course she had passed out rather quickly, but gulls in that condition were not unfamiliar to her.

"What difference does that make?" MacKay demanded.

"Seagulls," Elizabeth started softly, belying the revulsion she felt, "are often shot and the bodies tied to the roof antennae of lobster boats to discourage their brethren from hanging out and shitting all over the open cabins." MacKay looked as appalled as she had hoped. "Oak lath is the material from which better lobster traps are built. Dense wood. Heavy. Let me guess, Ginny, my gull was secured with copper nails." Ginny nodded. Frank cast an approving glance at his daughter and got himself another shot of cognac.

"What about the headstone on Debra Rothschilde's bed?" MacKay asked.

"Guilty," Eli offered, holding up his snifter for a refill. MacKay ignored him. "Found it in a pile of junk behind my cottage; figured to cast a little doubt in another direction. Pretty good, eh, Lizzie?"

The veins stuck out in Jesse's neck, but he stood by Frank in case the older man went ballistic. Frank stayed cool as a New Year's swim.

Eli continued, "Caught this little lady and her foxy sister trespassing and thought it might discourage any more amateur investigation. Guess I was off on that one. By the way, you got a cigarette I can bum?" Ginny pushed a pack across the table and tossed her lighter, which he caught tidily in his right hand. Elizabeth flashed to the face of Al Jenness; something about the knitted parlor head bound around his neck.

"Call me silly, Mr. Selby, but so far it seems you're guilty of everything. Can we cut to the chase, here? I'd just as soon have the Mass. troopers meet us at the dock," Ginny deadpanned.

"Fine with me," Eli agreed and tossed the cigarettes and lighter back to her. "It just so happens I was on one of my midnight runs over to visit the lovely, uh, Debra, was it? when I happened to notice a boat pulling traps. Or that's what I thought. You see I'm a city boy and didn't think it was that crazy to be out in the middle of the night gettin' the job done, you know? But I, personally, did not want to be seen, so I had to sit down in that spiky scrub grass shit and wait him out." He flicked an ash onto the floor. "Big brother already had me hiding my face from company earlier in the day, didn't you, Gary?"

"Is that right, Reverend?" Ginny turned her attention to the nauseated minister. Garrett Selby looked away, clearly unwilling to spill his guts without the benefit of an attorney. "Who was this mystery guest, Eli?"

"The guy who got himself whacked. Al Jenness."

"Of course!" Ginny smiled. "There is an entry in Jenness's desk diary for that day, Reverend. 'Cod.' Children of Deity. An unfortunate abbreviation, isn't it?"

The Reverend Selby made a squeaking noise deep in his throat, like a frightened mouse, but then found his famous voice. "We were discussing rental space for a soup kitchen in Portsmouth. After so many years in the community . . ."

As far as Elizabeth and Ginny knew, there were no homeless people in the area, and the hungry were already more than adequately cared for, as demonstrated by the frequency with which the Salvation Army closed for lack of needy.

"How did Jenness get out to the island?"

"I don't know, Chief, I honestly do not. I assumed he, well, he, uh, drove himself." Both women believed him. Most flatlanders thought all shore dwellers raced around on the water the way Angelenos took to the freeway.

"Well," Eli interjected, unwilling to give up center stage, "I *did* think it was peculiar that night that this guy comes out all this way just to tend one pot. Don't you?"

"Would you recognize the fisherman?"

"Nope, but it was definitely a man, and before you ask I probably wouldn't recognize the boat either—except I remember the name painted on the backside."

"Care to share it?" Ginny asked, pencil poised just as though she wouldn't remember whatever name he gave.

Elizabeth's mind raced.

"Nope. I'd just as soon be off this island before I give away my hand. You know?"

Ginny looked around the room. Five men, all viable suspects, Frank top of the list, Elizabeth written off at last. She stood and handcuffed Eli. "Frank and Jesse, we're going to head back to shore convoy-style. Frank, you take the lead and to my right, and I want you to make the *Curmudgeon* do some good time. Jesse, you're to my rear and left." The two men slid on their foul-weather gear without a word. Garrett Selby hunched where he had landed on entry. "Selby, you head back to Cap's or come along with your brother and me. I really don't care, just understand I'm not giving either of you a lift home."

Elizabeth wanted to scream with the pressure in her skull; writhing worms of thoughts banged around trying to reach fresh air. She convinced herself fresh air would do the trick.

"Ginny, do you have some heavier clothes I can borrow? I don't want to die on the way home."

Ginny turned to MacKay. "Think you can fix her up, MacKay?" He agreed. "Biz, I want you to spend the night here. Right now you're the only one I don't suspect of something, and I'd appreciate it if you could stay on Piscatawk and keep an eye on MacKay. He's a long shot, but I'd feel better." Ginny complimented herself on a fine piece of psychology.

"No way," Elizabeth said.

Ginny looked to Frank for support, though she did not feel she was owed any, under the circumstances.

"I'm restricting you to your room." He slapped his daughter on the shoulder. "Walk me to the dock, and if you're a good girl, I'll save you some lobster stew."

"I'm coming along," she insisted.

"You're grounded," Frank countered and slung his jacket over her shoulders for the walk to the water. "If I sleep late or anything, I'll send a water taxi out for you."

Elizabeth chose not to respond. She followed Ginny's entourage onto the dock and watched Jesse cast off, clumsy yet efficient as always. He always had to work hard to be as neat as he was; the injured hand did not slow him down a step.

Frank got into the skiff with Ginny, Garrett, and Eli for a ride to the *Curmudgeon,* still anchored behind Cap's Island. If it had been tied up with the *Celia T.,* Elizabeth would have jumped on board and it would have taken every available man to get her off, but she was unwilling to do that to poor old Jesse. He looked a hundred years old.

Though half frozen, from the dock she observed their slow progress around the tip of Piscatawk, and watched Frank boarding his old clunker. As instructed, he pulled away first headed to shore, followed by the other two boats. It was then that MacKay took her forcibly by the shoulders and led her back to the research station.

"My God," she said to the window through which she watched the *Curmudgeon* lumber south, "I don't even know who won the vote at the Town Meeting tonight." The police skiff rounded the island, keeping a safe but accessible distance.

"You did," MacKay informed her. "By a landslide."

Elizabeth was put out with herself that she just did not care. The evening should have been spent in celebration with Al: champagne, maybe some dancing. Instead, as soon as the *Celia T.* was out of sight, she was going to crawl into whatever bed was available and sink into a coma for a few hours.

"C'mon." MacKay nudged her. "I'll find you a bunk."

Elizabeth's limbs felt like redwoods, too heavy to move around. "Just a second." She swayed slightly and MacKay supported her without the expected condescension. Ginny must have her hands full in that little skiff, driving with one man in handcuffs and the other . . . The running lights of the *Celia T.* were not following. "Where's the *Celia T.?*"

"Kneeland's boat?" MacKay shrugged. "Maybe he had some trouble starting her up."

"Jesse? Never. He keeps that boat running like a surgical theater." Everything Jesse did was precision, despite . . . "Oh, my God." Elizabeth spun out of MacKay's warm arms and ran out of the lounge and back into Debra's wrecked room, MacKay on her heels. She dashed past the bed, slamming her foot into the headstone on the floor, and thrust her head out the window without taking the time to appreciate the toe she'd broken. "Shit!"

MacKay leaned over her back to see what she was looking at. "What is it?"

"The *Celia T.*" she pointed to the running lights growing dimmer in the distance, headed out to sea. "What kind of a boat do you have? Power?" She vaguely remembered an ESG craft bobbing at the east side of the dock when the others boarded. "Never mind." She pushed past MacKay as fast as she could. MacKay followed easily.

"Wait a minute, he's heading straight out, not even toward the other shoals. There's nothing out there but open sea."

No one knew that better than Elizabeth Will; and no one knew Jesse Kneeland better than she did, either. She hit the exterior doors with a bang and hobbled painfully over the crushed shell and rock pathway to the dock. MacKay grabbed her as she struggled with the knots that secured the lab's runabout. She shook him off without loosing her fingers from the rope, her enormous strength fired by adrenaline. He repositioned himself, braced, and lifted her off her feet. Rather than struggle, she relaxed every muscle until he set her back on the splintery wood.

"We have to go after him," she said urgently, her eyes locked on his. "You don't know Jesse. You don't know what it means."

"We'll call Chief Philbrick from the office."

Elizabeth's mind raced. "Right. Right. But we'll call from the boat. We have to get to Jesse *now*." She saw the dark-haired man consider, waver. "*Please* trust me. I didn't know until now, *please*." MacKay dropped his hands and Elizabeth jumped down into the boat, fingers releasing the final loop on the knot as he dropped down behind her. "Keys under the seat?" she asked at the same moment she found them and started the engine. The powerful motor drowned out whatever response her unwilling companion might have made. She pushed away from the pilings and threw the transmission into reverse so rapidly that MacKay lost his tenuous footing and tumbled backward into the rear seats. The double-engine craft flew gratifyingly across the water. Elizabeth lifted the mike from its cradle and handed it on its coiled wire to MacKay behind her. "You wanna call? Call."

MacKay fumbled the mouthpiece, the tension from the cord pulling it through the front bucket seats, where he retrieved it and shouted for Ginny. He was not certain the CB was set to the correct frequency, but was not willing to risk falling overboard to get to the main unit. When Ginny answered, he shouted the situation above the blast of the engines over his shoulder. Before he signed off, Elizabeth plucked the mike from his hand and disengaged it. The *Celia T.* was just ahead, plowing through the larger and larger swells the way Jesse Kneeland plugged through life: strong, steady, without imagination.

Tears flattened across Elizabeth's face like rain on a windshield. Poor Jesse. How could she have accused *him* of having no imagination when she herself had been handed every clue available and had still failed to put together the story. The knitted head wrapped around Al's neck had been knotted backwards—left-handed and with cotton twine. The morning Jesse showed up before the Coast Guard to comfort her, the hood of his sweatshirt had been flapping around. Because the cording was missing. That's why his ears had been so red. He had removed the tie from his hood to close the opening in the parlor head.

The cabin of the *Celia T.* came clearly into view, as clean as a nursery, the seagull carcass gone from the marine radio antenna. How could she have been so stupid? Everyone in town had thought she and Al were fooling around and she'd been too proud to deny it, even if it was almost true. Jesse must have taken it man to man that night after the Town Meeting . . . Elizabeth matched the speed of the *Celia T.* and pulled as close to the side as was safe—about a foot. The *Celia* was pulling slightly westward, no captain at the helm.

"Take the wheel," she ordered MacKay. He had grabbed the back of her seat and was trying to pull himself into the bow of the moving craft. "Take the wheel!" Elizabeth balanced upright, putting most of her weight on her undamaged right foot. As MacKay reached to pull her back into the seat, she got hold of a metal securing T-bar on the rail of Jesse's boat, and MacKay's hand slipped off the fistful of rugby shirt. "Match speed and pull aside!"

Elizabeth slapped her free hand over the one clawed around the T-bar, flexed her right thigh, and threw the foot with the broken toe over the rail of the *Celia T.* Using the swinging arc of her right leg as propulsion, she flipped onto her face on the slatted decking and immediately scrabbled to her knees. With a quick movement, she threw the engine into neutral and heard MacKay's vessel pull ahead.

More than anything in the world, Elizabeth wanted to see Jesse sprawled on the aft deck, but she was not surprised to see nothing except his meticulously entered log book laid like an Aztec sacrifice on the altar of a white beer cooler. Jesse was not on board. In the distance she could hear the yowl of the siren on the police skiff.

NINETEEN

THE DOVEKEY BEACH police station was really just the second floor of a small Victorian cottage set between the Town Hall and new brick volunteers' firehouse on the main street. The first floor served as civil court and judge's chambers. Since there were no facilities for prisoners, the rare few arrested were shipped over to Portsmouth or Hampton, with special guests going to the county jail in Exeter. Eli made the big time by New Hampshire standards.

The trip back from the islands was silent, but Eli Selby had said plenty on the aborted voyage before Jesse Kneeland's disappearance. It was, indeed, the *Celia T.* he had seen the night of the murder. He also contended that Al Jenness had made his trip to visit the Reverend Garrett Selby to inform him of a glitch in his ownership of the hotel retreat. Blackmail, Ginny surmised, which was confirmed by the minister himself in the presence of his attorney. Ruth Jenness had merely been following up in her office the day Ginny saw the two of them together there with the architectural studies. Regardless of who owned the island, the lease on the land had expired in 1980.

Jesse's last log entry was hastily entered, as he was well aware that his veering off course would not go unnoticed for long. It read in his tortured hand:

Lizzie,

It was an accident, I promise, Al just fell and I didnt kill him but nobody would believe it so I sent him down—didnt even know it was Frank's pot when I grabbed it. Honest. He was going to use you to get ahold of Caps but it was an accident. We was just going to talk. Im so sorry but I fixed what I could. I love you Lizzie. Hope you like your present.

PS: Look at the church registry on Caps if you cant find your bible.

It was not signed.

Avis wept so uncontrollably at that detail that Ginny handed her the phone to try her mother one more time, though she had ceased worrying much over Sal's whereabouts. Sal picked up on the first ring, chastised her daughter for waking her so early in the morning when she was still jet-lagged from her romance convention in Monte Carlo, insisted she had told just *everyone* about going, and promised to call back as soon as she had her beauty sleep. Elizabeth shook her head to prevent Avis from spinning the entire story on the phone.

Avis's piles of documentation spread on Ginny's desk seemed to prove that the Will family were, after all, the legal owners of Cap's Island. This the Reverend Selby vehemently denied.

"The family left the island and negated the conditions of the original grant," he asserted firmly. "I have the parson's journal that gives the dates Thomas and Lydia Will moved off the island."

"May I see it?" Ginny asked.

"Of course. But it's on the island, naturally. It's not the kind of thing a person carries around with him."

"Naturally," Ginny agreed. "It will save a lot of time and another trip for you if you'll agree to let the Coasties bring it over here right now. They're out there anyway searching for Jesse's body."

"Of course," Garrett answered readily. The sun was weeping through the muslin-draped windows of Ginny's office. He would miss the first service, but might make it for grace before the noon meal. "I left it on my desk. May I use your phone to authorize the Coast Guard to remove it?" Ginny nodded and handed him the old-fashioned black rotary telephone. "Sister Mary? This is Reverend Selby . . . Are you in the library? Good. On my desk is an old book . . . Right on top. It's a worn leather . . . Mary, it's the only book *on* the desk." The color drained from Selby's already sallow face. "No, I'm sure it's not. Mary, some Coast Guard people may be visiting our island this morning. Please extend them every courtesy. Yes, the library especially. Thank you, Sister, I hope to be home by the afternoon service." He hung up the receiver and spoke to Ginny. "I swear to you, it was all written in that book. It's impossible, but the book has disappeared."

"Not impossible at all," Frank said. "I expect when I sent Jesse over to Cap's to look for my pain-in-the-ass daughter here, he took it. Guess if you ever pull him up, you'll find it, all right."

"You've seen the journal?" Elizabeth asked, aghast.

"Nope," Frank answered. "But I believe it's true."

"You *want* to believe it," Elizabeth accused.

"Damn right," he answered calmly. MacKay looked over at Frank Will as though he had never seen him before. Elizabeth ground her teeth, trying to control herself and listen to what her father had to say. "There has never been a Will daughter that lived into adulthood on that island. Not ever. I saw my own sister die out there and that was enough for me. Too much. You want to see the family Bible, Liz? It's in the hold of the *Curmudgeon* and what it lists is three hundred years of dead baby girls. When your mother entered your name at the end of that list, my mother made me swear you would never see that island and, by gawd, I kept my word. By gawd, I did." Frank Will's eyes narrowed grotesquely, seeing nothing in the brightening room. Avis leaned nearer her father.

"We're grown now, Dad," Elizabeth said accusingly.

Frank picked a cigarette from Ginny's pack on the desk and lit it, inhaling to the bottom of his lungs. He marveled at the burning end, twisting the cigarette back and forth between his thick fingers. He pronounced each word as though it had been handed down from the Mount. "You are my baby girls. Mine." A monster tear fell from Avis's eye and dropped onto Frank's sleeve. He took another drag of the cigarette and stubbed it out. "Live with it."

MacKay was the first to speak. "Is there any reason I can't go back to Piscatawk, Chief Philbrick?"

Ginny swiped at the tip of her nose with the heel of her hand. "Not that I can think of. Selby, I want you here until the Coasties get what they get, but everyone else can go."

MacKay nodded his good-byes and went to the door. Ginny stopped Elizabeth as she started after him.

"The letters were burned, Biz."

"What letters, Ginny? I don't want to hear another word about paperwork today, okay?"

Ginny lowered her voice. "The letters you wrote to Al. Ruth found them and, rather than raise a scandal, she just burned them." Elizabeth listened carefully for a full thirty seconds after Ginny had stopped talking. Then she reacted with a distinctly raunchy guffaw.

Elizabeth whispered into Ginny's ear. "I never wrote any letters, Gin. I thought a lot about grabbing something cheap and physical with Al, but nothing more than an experimental kiss here or there. Ruth lied to you about any letters."

"Why?" Ginny asked.

"Damned if I know, and at this moment I truly could not care less. That's your job, right?"

"Right."

Elizabeth limped quickly down the flight of stairs and outside into a perfect early-summer morning. She shouted to MacKay at his van.

"Hey! Thanks for the loan of the shirt. I'll wash it and get it back to you," she said.

"Keep it," MacKay answered. "It never looked that good on me."

"Thanks, and MacKay?" she asked, hobbling over to where he stood.

"Yes?"

"Can I call you sometime later in the week?"

MacKay kept a straight face, despite the unexpected boost to his ego. "If you like, that would be fine."

"Good," Elizabeth asserted. "I'd like to get started organizing the opposition to the island gambling bill before it gets presented to the legislature. Dad blew it because he's just too damned bombastic." She smacked him heartily on the arm and turned back to the door with weary determination.

Avis's husband would finally prove useful in the endless court appearances to come, the death inquest and challenges she planned to launch for full title to Cap's Island. MacKay could almost see the wheels turning as he watched her limp stiffly, posture perfect, away from him.

"Oh." Elizabeth interrupted her own thoughts and looked over her shoulder. "And if you're free tonight, MacKay, why don't you drop by the house." She finished with a sardonic curl at one corner of her mouth. "Unless I miss my guess, there ought to be enough lobster stew to feed an army."